I0671791

Uncertainty Principles

A NOVEL

Krista Tibbs

Published in the United States
by Friction Publishing, Tennessee

Friction Publishing Trade Paperback
2019 Revised Edition

ISBN: 978-0-9818803-7-2

Printed in the United States of America

10 9 8 7 6 5 4 3 2

UNCERTAINTY
PRINCIPLES

I

THE MONTHS OF OUR REUNION BEGAN WITH ONE LETTER. The letter that Brian sent three times in two weeks. The one that Aiyana threw away, as she had done to all of the others for the past nine years. The envelope drifted slightly to the right, possibly detoured by a random particle appearing from nothing—an odd fact of physics, no miracle required. The force of gravity pulled it to the floor, although my Becky might say there was a divine force also.

If Aiyana had never looked, there would still be a story, just not this one. Until she opened the envelope, both annihilation and redemption were possible and the future was uncertain.

Aiyana abhorred uncertainty.

Neither Becky nor Aiyana was a big drinker, but the night of Brian's letter, the two of them went to the town pub, The Foehn. An unusually large crowd filled the entranceway, and as they waited to get in, Becky read the plaque on the door.

> *Foehns are the witches' winds that blow across the world: Santa Ana,*
> *Khamsin, Diablo, Chinook, Zonda, and Viento Sur, to name a few.*
> *The best cure for a hot, ill wind is a cold, wet beer.*
>
> **Welcome to The Foehn.**
>
> *Judgment is reserved when a Sirocco is in season.*

A woman behind her said, "I don't know about witches, but I wish it would rain already. This never-ending overcast is making people crazy." The truth of the statement still makes Becky shiver.

Aiyana pulled Becky through the masses of people and ordered a Bavarian Blue Haze and a Zephyrus. They didn't even get a taste because the television above the bar flashed a newsbreak about a road rage incident that ended in a triple murder in a town outside San Jose. Becky said, "Alum Rock," a second before *Alum Rock, California* appeared on the screen.

"How did you know?" Aiyana asked. She must have already suspected.

"Brian predicted it."

Brian didn't send Becky his letter that day or the other two before it. If he had, she would have opened them right away, as always. Always. She read every one of his words, every number, every graph, whether or not she understood them.

"Inside fifty miles?"

"Inside ten miles. And within the week."

Aiyana had never believed Brian could reach such accuracy. That was part of the reason she had thrown away all of his envelopes marked "Prediction" then "Confirmation". She did believe he was a coward, to know those things would happen and do nothing about it. He hadn't published his work. He couldn't even tell Becky about the prediction that was burning a hole in Aiyana's purse.

I have often wondered why Aiyana finally opened Brian's letter. She must have picked up the envelope and hesitated, curious to know why it was the third one in two weeks. She probably slid her pretentious glass letter opener under the flap before she realized what she was doing. She never allowed herself to be absent-minded, but maybe a weird dream the night before had put her in a mood. Maybe a patient had developed an illness in spite of her instructions. Maybe she had been distracted by Becky's text: *Dinner tonight? We're getting a baby.* A period, not an exclamation point. Not like Becky at all.

In any case, once she flipped through the pages, the story was chosen. She couldn't unread the graphs showing the increasing likelihood of catastrophe, or unsee the tragic photos of foreshadowing events, or misunderstand their meaning, made explicit by the handwritten note: *Pattern suggests major violence centered in Freedom, Kansas the week of June 2nd.*

It was the first day of March.

Aiyana knew the quantum law, that there is no such thing as just an observer. Once she looked, she became part of the outcome, even if she took no action at all. I like to imagine the thoughts that ran through her mind: *gutless invertebrate, Heisenberg ostrich, lily-livered meteorological pretty boy.* We always did think highly of Brian.

2

Nine Years Earlier

Soteriophobia: Fear of dependence on others

Aiyana's long legs carried her swiftly across the student lounge toward the corner where the senior project team would meet for the first time. Her mahogany skin crawled with irritation when she felt two fraternity boys ogling her from the hallway.

Someone was already waiting on the couch. That must be Becky, Aiyana thought. The girl was wearing a gray sweatshirt, and her hair reminded Aiyana of something... Pudding. Yes, like the school bully had dumped a bowl of vanilla pudding on her head, and she let it happen.

Aiyana sighed and put on a smile before she stepped around the couch, stuck out her hand, and announced herself. "Where's"—she checked her phone for the name of the Rocks for Jocks major who had arranged the meeting—"Brian?" He had signed the email *Brian Richter (no relation, though I'm an 8).* Apparently, earthquake jokes passed for humor in geology class.

"Right behind you," said a male voice.

Aiyana caught a clean smell and turned to see exactly what she had imagined, a freshly showered locker room poster boy. Not simply the boy next door but the boy at the center of the beach party, sandy hair and all. Great.

"Sorry I'm late. I just got out of practice. So, which one of you is the pre-med?" he said.

Aiyana almost laughed. Wasn't it obvious? "Pre-med and electrical engineering," she said.

"Oh, you've been taking it easy here." He beamed a smile toward her, and she was annoyed at herself for feeling flattered. He turned to the blond girl. "That means you're Becky, the soon-to-be teacher." Becky blushed, and then she asked him something in a voice too soft for Aiyana to tolerate for the rest of the semester. He leaned over and asked her to repeat it.

"Baseball," he answered, standing up. "First year for the sport here at New Tech. We're playing an exhibition game down in Topeka next week. Wish us luck!" He cocked his head to the side and squinted at Aiyana. She steeled herself for some charming remark. Instead, he said, "You and I were in a class together."

"I don't think so." She wouldn't even take a nap in one of his weatherman classes.

"It was Advanced Materials. Your presentation used copper in a thermoelectric couple, and I thought you could get a more stable resistance with a copper-nickel alloy, but we never got a chance to talk about it because the guy before you ran way over his time."

"Oh." Aiyana tried to reconcile her first impression with this new intelligence.

He winked. "The Earth and Atmospheric Science Program—it's not your typical Rocks for Jocks."

Aiyana laughed in surprise. Was she that transparent?

"What's so funny?" The fraternity boy walking toward them had on a tight black t-shirt, and Aiyana thought the muscles underneath were decent, for a short guy. He shook Brian's hand first. "I'm Kai Inoue. Kai as in fly. Thanks for setting this up, man." His black marble eyes gave Aiyana the once-over, and any attraction she might have felt dissipated immediately. He plopped onto the couch next to Becky. "Hi there."

Becky squeezed her hands in her lap and emitted a silent hello. Aiyana rolled her eyes. "Does anyone know this other guy, Dmitri?"

No one knew of him, and he hadn't answered Brian's e-mail. Before Aiyana could suggest they start without him, Kai said, "Hey, what do you guys do for fun?" He and Brian launched into a conversation about sports, and Brian took a seat on the couch on the other side of Becky. Aiyana didn't feel the need to contribute to the niceties, so she pulled up a metal chair to observe them across the coffee table. Brian oozed charisma, and compared to him, Kai was plastic, like a Japanese Ken doll. He would probably wear the title proudly. Between the two boys, Becky gradually shrank in upon herself and alternated between blush and pallor as though she couldn't decide whether to flee or disappear.

After twenty minutes of meaningless chitchat, Dmitri arrived. His rusty helmet of uncombed hair was the second thing they noticed. The first was his purple cape lined in silver, which he twirled with a flourish over his dark jeans, too skinny on his paunchy frame and an inch too short to meet his flat gray Converse sneakers manufactured circa the 1970s. Beneath his cape, he wore a wrinkled t-shirt printed with the text: *My questions are for your benefit. I already know the answers.* They all stared up at him, speechless. He said, "I am Dmitri. Let us begin."

3

March 1: 51%

I know Aiyana had many suspicions that night at the pub. But she couldn't tell Becky about them, not while Becky's hand still clutched the note I had left by our bedside that morning: *We can't raise a baby in today's world.*

Even Aiyana recognized the unfairness of what I had done, after such a long wait on the adoption list. She couldn't believe the timing was mere coincidence. She left the pub and went outside to focus her thoughts, but there was no fresh air. Positive ions clogged the sky, hanging heavily beneath the ever-approaching storm. She opened the letter again to the map centered on Freedom, Kansas, where the danger to her patients was laid out in black and red.

Aiyana's medical practice had grown each year largely thanks to Becky's referrals, from our neighbor with his high blood pressure and weakness for barbecue to the assistant principal whose passion for meditating stressed her out. Aiyana wasn't connected to the community like Becky; to her, Freedom was little more than the place she had landed because it needed a doctor enough to lure her straight out of residency.

However, she did have an overdeveloped sense of responsibility, so it bothered her that Brian could sit on high in his academic office and follow up his predictions in a few months with an envelope marked, "Confirmed", enclosed with clippings telling the story of whatever catastrophe had befallen her charges. I think what bothered her more was how fate could trump all of her preventive medicine.

"Those chicken shits," she said. I always enjoyed Aiyana's lapses in vocabulary; in the beginning, they were my only inkling that she might be human.

"Aiyana!" Becky had followed her to the porch. "Did you come out here to swear? You're like a smoker who can't quit."

"I have no intention of quitting." Aiyana folded the letter and slipped it into her pocket. "Grab a toothbrush, Becky; we're going on a road trip. I know how to find your husband."

There was a flash of lightning and a crack of thunder, and an unseasonably warm wind followed them to the car.

4

Decidophobia: Fear of decision-making

Dmitri sat in the deep windowsill with his cape draped around him, half hiding the words on his t-shirt: *Perception is reality*. One finger repeatedly flicked the shiny silver window lock. Aiyana was pacing the length of the dorm room, and Brian was leaning back in a desk chair with his feet in white crew socks propped against the wall. Kai had left to answer his phone again. Becky decided to take the empty soda cans to the recycling bin to avoid hearing Aiyana complain about how little Kai contributed. She had made it perfectly clear that slackers were unwelcome on her team.

Maybe Kai wasn't ambitious, Becky thought, but she felt like the dead weight on their project. They were supposed to come up with a real world problem to be solved as a team, so Becky had suggested organizing a community watch to keep kids safe from bullies. Aiyana had dismissed it as fluffy, and Dmitri had just said no. Brian had been more gracious about it because he really was an awfully nice guy. He had reminded her that the assignment required them to include all of their fields of study, and he couldn't see how his geology skills would be much value in walking kids home from school. Becky appreciated his kindness, but she was sure he thought her to be an idiot as much as Aiyana and Dmitri obviously did.

Their cross-functional project was the only requirement left for graduation, and they would pass or fail as a team—a randomly assigned team. As far as Becky could tell, they were on a path toward failing.

Oh dear, Aiyana's pessimism was rubbing off on her. The cans clattered down the recycling chute, and Becky headed toward the bathroom to wash her hands.

At first, coming up with a problem had been kind of fun because there were no limitations, but frustration had set in when they realized they couldn't prove the causes of global warming, stop school bullying, or cure cancer in two semesters. They decided to consider smaller, more local concerns. Kai had suggested "market research". He often threw out business terms like that, and Becky was never sure what they meant in practice. She didn't think he knew either because usually Brian and Aiyana came up with the specifics. However, for market research, Kai went on to explain how they could ask companies if any community issues were affecting their business, which would give the team a list to pick from. Aiyana proclaimed that she had no interest in selling her degree to the highest bidder. Becky didn't say so out loud, but she agreed. Designing their major project around money and companies and markets would somehow taint her diploma.

By the time Becky returned to Brian's room, Kai had also returned. "We have a long list of problems, but nothing we can solve before the end of the year, if ever," Brian was saying.

Becky's heart felt heavy with their catalogue of human suffering.

"That's not going to get me to graduation," Aiyana said.

"It is a weakness, your fear of defeat," Dmitri said. "Kakorrhaphiophobia."

Aiyana squinted as though she could focus her irritation into a laser that would evaporate Dmitri.

"I've been working on something we might be able to adapt." Brian swung his feet to the floor and sat up in his chair. His knee bounced as he described his independent research. "I think I have a model and enough past data to predict when the next earthquake of Richter scale seven or above is going to hit North America. It requires a magnetometer upgrade, so I could definitely use some help with the physics." He looked over at Dmitri, who was reading the newspaper. "Becky, we'd need a good education program. Kai, there are certainly business aspects in getting funded." Kai shrugged. Becky nodded.

"What am I supposed to do, stand around and look pretty?" Aiyana said.

Brian flashed a big grin. "You can do whatever your pretty little heart desires. Emphasis on the little."

Becky admired him for being slow to anger, for not letting someone else's bad attitude faze him. Aiyana crossed her arms and leaned against the wardrobe. "So, our paper is going to be about how early and how well we can tell people to run away? I don't see that as a solution to a problem."

"Define the problem," Dmitri said.

"Duh, the earthquake?" Aiyana said.

"Challenge your assumptions." The others waited for Dmitri to explain, but he continued reading the paper as though he had only been talking to himself.

Brian picked up a piece of purple granite from his desk. "Do you think planetariums show pictures of asteroids and bursting suns and other far-off doom for the express purpose of scaring people?"

"Yes, and I think the tradition is marvelous," Aiyana said. "It make kids more responsible, tree-hugging, universe-contemplating, ozone-seeing adults, and gives them comfort that one day everyone they despise will burn up into space debris. It is a vital part of the national culture." A rare smile tickled the corner of Aiyana's lips.

"Well, Becky, we've solved your bullying problem after all. More trips to the planetarium!" Becky did love Brian's laugh. "They do it"—he tossed the purple rock to Aiyana, who caught it with ease —"to remind us of the natural events we have to live around, like the weather. We can't change the weather, so we predict it. The problem isn't the weather itself, or the earthquakes; the problem is our response, how we communicate the threat, how we deal with an issue we can't control."

"I'd prefer a problem I *can* control."

"Of course you would."

Becky liked the camaraderie between Aiyana and Brian. She envied it, but she was also grateful; it was the one thing holding their team together. She couldn't come so far and not graduate. She couldn't live down to her mother's expectations.

"Perhaps we can change the atmosphere." Dmitri jumped down from the windowsill, and his newspaper fluttered to the floor. Below the front-page story about a student in a coma, the headline "Physics lab dangerous for students?" accompanied an article and a vignette box at the bottom of the page. The box contained a quote from the Students Of Safety: "We don't know the answer because no one will do the study."

"Brian, your research depends on electromagnetic fields, yes?"

"More or less."

"Then we will do the study." Again, they waited for Dmitri to explain. He pointed to the newspaper.

Aiyana snatched it up and scanned silently while the others watched her. Becky expected a snide remark, but instead, a smile spread across her face. "They think the particle accelerator in the physics building is going to give us all cancer."

Becky didn't consider cancer anything to smile about.

"I don't get it," Kai said, looking back down at his phone.

Brian turned to Becky. "It's like a house underneath a power line. They're worried that the electromagnetic field generated by the physics lab is too strong to be near the student center."

"Shouldn't the physics students *in* the lab be more worried?" Becky aimed her question at Dmitri.

He shrugged. "It is not a problem."

Becky was still confused, but she resigned herself to it, stifling any further questions. Brian continued to explain. "What he means is that we should forget about earthquakes and use the magnetometers to measure the EMF field around the physics building compared to the student lounge and other areas on campus. If we show there's no electromagnetic difference, then we show there's no danger."

"No, we have to try to prove there *is* a difference," Aiyana said.

"There is no problem," Dmitri said, his voice a bit louder.

"But we have to *operate* as if there were. We can't propose a final paper on a non-problem." She grabbed a notebook from Kai's lap. He reached for it, but she flipped it open and leaned over Brian's desk. Becky noticed the notebook was empty. Aiyana said, "If all we plan to do is provide data that shows nothing, the only thing we'll accomplish is shutting up the protestors. That might be a courtesy to the student body, but it's not a graduation-worthy effort."

Brian smiled. "You're saying data collection and hypothesis testing are just *part* of the project; the real work is determining how we'll communicate the problem and handle the response."

Kai said, "A risk management plan."

"Exactly." Aiyana was rapidly writing lists into the notebook. "We will propose to collect data in order to convince people to do something about the location of the student lounge. In the meantime, we'll prepare an education program"—she ripped off a page and passed it to Becky—"about the medical implications of strong EMF. We'll prepare a financial analysis"—she tossed the notebook back to Kai, knocking the phone from his hand—"of what it would cost and how long it would take to move the lounge compared to the long-term costs of not doing so. Then…" She leaned back against the wall and crossed her arms. "Then we end the paper with our real data, which Dmitri is convinced will show no difference. If he's wrong, we'll have the risk management plan to fall back on, but if he's right, then we'll be done. Either way, we graduate. Agreed?"

Becky voiced agreement, but in her mind, there was one thought: What is a magnetometer?

5

Macrophobia: Fear of long waits

"We could write a book," Aiyana said as she stood up from the floor of Brian's dorm room and stretched. "The topic would be how to rein in an arrogant ass. We'd call it *Waiting for Dmitri*."

Laughing, Brian grabbed another root beer from the micro fridge. He offered one to Becky, who was perched on the bottom bunk, but she shook her head demurely. Why did she do that? Aiyana wondered. The girl was obviously thirsty; she'd been swallowing every three seconds since they got there.

It had been nearly a week since they had decided on a project, and they were ready to distribute the magnetometers around campus and start measuring the electromagnetic fields. Dmitri hadn't been on time for a team meeting yet, and it was anyone's guess whether he'd show up ten minutes late or forty-five. The others talked about meaningless things while Aiyana kept checking the clock. The waste was maddening. Plus, Becky's obvious crush on Brian was growing by the minute. No good could come of that.

"Hey, I found out something about Dmitri," Brian said in a hushed tone. "His father is Andrey Chesnokov."

"Who's that?" Kai asked, engrossed in his phone, per usual.

"Who cares?" Aiyana said.

Brian said, "He's a nuclear physicist."

"So? We already know the kid's a friggin' genius."

"I'm talking about the Russian physicist who sold climate data to the U.S. government and is now rotting in a Siberian prison."

Aiyana heard the echo of a childhood fear. *Daddy, why do the policemen follow you around? Are you going to get arrested? Don't worry, my Aiyana; they're just doing their jobs.*

Kai lifted his head, engaged for the first time that day. "I remember my parents talking about him when I was a kid. Didn't he sell the top secret data to a bunch of other countries, too?"

"So, he deserved to go to prison?" Aiyana said. *Dad, why don't you get angry when strangers act nervous around you? You don't deserve to be treated like a criminal. Aiyana, anger is a choice.*

Brian shook his head. "That's what the headlines said, but if you read further, there's more to the story. From what I can tell, his father had data showing how the Russian government's early attempts at weather modification created monster storms that decimated parts of the U.S. coastline. The military wanted to use the information to create a climate weapon, but he spoke out against it and threatened to publish his findings. He applied for amnesty here when he heard the Russian government was going to shut him up somehow. The U.S.

government pressured him to hand over his data, too, supposedly to recoup the cost of the damages, but Chesnokov was skeptical, so he sold the information to both the U.S. and several other countries in order to neutralize the military potential. His amnesty was only temporary, so eventually he was extradited back to Russia to stand trial for treason."

"Then why is Dmitri here?" Aiyana asked, thinking maybe he should go back where he belonged.

"Chesnokov's price to the U.S. government was climate data in exchange for expedited citizenship for his eight-year-old son. Before he got deported, he set his son up at a Catholic children's home in Cloud County, Kansas. Fitting, huh?"

"Dmitri was here all alone?" Becky's heart was on her sleeve for the world to see, per usual. "At least when my dad left, I still had my mom."

Aiyana said, "No wonder he's so weird."

"He wasn't alone; he was in the orphanage," Brian said.

"Didn't he have any other family in Russia?"

"No." They all looked toward the voice in the doorway, unaware of how long Dmitri had been standing there. His eyes, like two gray doves, surveyed them, unblinking.

The awkwardness stretched until Aiyana broke and said, "About time you got here. We're three weeks into the semester, and we haven't started the damn project yet. I refuse to allow you to get between me and my summa cum laude." She grabbed five of the electromagnetic devices that Brian had borrowed from the geology lab and handed them to Dmitri.

The other teammates also launched into motion, clearing their throats of the intrusive conversation. Brian said, "We need one as close as you can get to the accelerator, plus somewhere else in the physics lab, on the lawn behind the building, a hundred feet away, and two hundred feet away, right?"

"That's farther into campus than you've ventured over the past three years, isn't it, Dmitri?" Aiyana asked.

Dmitri pointed to his t-shirt: *My sense of humor is appropriate to context.* He took the devices and left the dorm room.

"Does that mean he was amused?" Aiyana said to Becky.

Becky said, "I don't know, but I was." Aiyana almost smiled. The two had come to something of a truce: Becky didn't try to pretend she was intelligent, and Aiyana didn't try to pretend she was nice. Oddly, the more Becky spoke up, the less Aiyana felt the need to intimidate her, which eased the tension.

Aiyana took one of the magnetometers from her bag and turned over the phone-like object in her hands. It was supposed to collect data on the field strength out to a hundred feet. She doubted that anything the earth and atmospheric sciences department could procure by the dozens would be strong enough to detect a difference between locations, even if there was one. However, since she was sure there was no difference to detect, it didn't much matter. Aiyana put the device back in her bag with the others and left to place them at her targets around the medical facility.

Brian and Becky took the remaining devices to the student lounge. Becky didn't feel as special as she usually did when Brian asked her to assist him because she knew he was trying to make up for Aiyana hijacking her assigned task. For days, Becky had been working up the courage to ask permission to conduct their project, until Aiyana *happened* to be in the professor's office and did it herself.

As they walked across the quad, ducking frisbees and skirting students cramming for the year's first set of exams, Becky asked Brian, "How do these work, anyway?"

"Well, there are different kinds of magnetometers," he said, assuming his teaching assistant voice, patient but authoritative. That voice acted had the effect of a uniform on Becky's growing attraction. "This one works by emitting a small electric charge. The EMF in the area—electromagnetic field, I mean—will put pressure on the test charge to align with the field. The stronger the field, the stronger the pressure, and therefore, the higher the voltage we calculate. When we take readings from a variety of locations, we can basically map the relative strength of the EMFs around campus."

"Wouldn't they be affected just by people walking by? A person has an energy field, too, right?"

"People do have bioelectricity of sorts, but it's nothing compared to the magnetism in the atmosphere. So anything that the meters pick up from people will be part of the background noise, which we're going to factor out."

Brian checked to make sure no one was watching, and then tucked the device into a corner of the couch. Becky studied the golden haze emanating beyond his skin. It was hard for her to believe that an energy field she could see was weaker than one she couldn't even feel. Of course, she didn't really *feel* gravity because she'd never been without it.

"How do people get cancer from electricity and magnets?" she asked. She followed behind Brian as they navigated the furniture to measure the length between their hiding spots.

"You'd have to ask Aiyana about that. I haven't taken biology since high school!"

Becky had no intention of asking Aiyana. "Does the electricity pass through people?"

"Well, anything with a positive or negative charge is possibly a conductor, as you know." She nodded, although she didn't know any such thing. "Metal is the best conductor, of course, and when you put a piece of metal in an electromagnetic field, it will turn toward the direction of the field, like our test charges." Brian stopped walking and talked aloud as though he were figuring out the answer. "Since our bodies are full of atoms with electrons and protons, when we enter an electromagnetic field, it could adjust our charges, realign them, take a few electrons or give a few electrons and create positive or negative ions." He hid another device behind a curtain.

Becky said, "Are ions bad for your health?"

"Like I said, you'd have to ask Aiyana about the biology behind it, but I have read that some people swear they get sick from the Santa Ana winds, which carry positive ions. On the flip side, after it rains, the air is usually full of negative ions. I don't know about you, but I think that feels good."

Becky remembered her mental image of Brian on the first day they met: a country road after a summer shower. Yes, it felt really good.

They hid their last device in the bush outside the bottom floor window of the student building. "That's all of them," Brian said. "Now we wait for whatever happens."

6

March 1: 53%

One thing I always liked about Aiyana—well, "like" may be a strong word—was her ability to say anything on her mind. The night she and Becky left the pub in search of me, after an hour of driving with Becky staring in silence out the window, Aiyana had no trouble asking, "Do you love him?"

Becky hesitated. She was probably wondering which one of us Aiyana meant by "him".

"I mean, do you like being married?" Aiyana had never understood marriage, not even the concept of it. She had never known anyone with whom she wanted to share her space, let alone her life, or her world views.

"Sometimes." Becky's answer was true for both questions.

The conversation stopped there while Aiyana navigated past a minor fender bender. Two drivers stood on the shoulder of the road, facing each other with silent movie expressions of rage while their families watched through steamy windows.

The road was jammed with people trying to get away, honking in general frustration at the obstacles. Each passing headlight glared briefly in the rearview mirror like a sad and distant supernova.

7

Ecclesiophobia: Fear of church

After a week of observations near the physics lab, Becky's email pinged with a new message from Brian: *Hey guys, take a look at this.* She opened the attachment. It was a graph of the data they had collected.

Becky's job had been to collate the readings from all of the magnetometers into Brian's database, which Brian then used to create graphs and tables for analysis. The graph in the attachment showed the average readings in each location at different points of the day. In the mess of squiggly lines, Becky could see that one of them spiked at about seven o'clock on Monday evening. She thought she had noticed it in the data, but because there were so many numbers and they varied so much, she hadn't said anything out loud. The second graph Brian sent also showed a spike about the same time on Tuesday. It had happened every day for the past four days.

Let's meet outside the medical center at 6:45 after Aiyana's shift and find out what's going on. -Brian

When Becky arrived at the medical center, Aiyana and Brian were already there. "If Dmitri and knucklehead don't show up in two minutes, I'm going without them," Aiyana said.

Becky didn't like how Aiyana disparaged Kai. He wasn't such a bad guy. Becky was intimidated by him, as she was by most people, but she also related to him. The two of them were merely hangers-on in Brian and Aiyana's project and peasants at the feet of Dmitri's great intellect. Sometimes Becky wondered why she bothered trying. She had also started to think that Kai wasn't as lazy as Aiyana thought, because he was always busy with something, although it wasn't usually their project.

"Okay, it's six forty-seven. I'm going."

Becky and Brian followed Aiyana through the lobby, out the revolving door, and along the brick wall of the building. Becky felt weird about skulking around in the night, especially at a hospital, but she kept telling herself it was what they had to do to graduate.

They heard voices, and Aiyana stopped. She tossed a questioning glance back at Brian, who shrugged his shoulders. One voice was louder than the others. "Hey guys, sorry I haven't been here this week. How's she doing?"

"Better," someone answered.

Aiyana gestured them over to the bushes, where they crouched to watch a circle of people sitting on the ground, holding hands. A flashlight in the middle of the circle illuminated the closed eyes and worried brows. The circle fell quiet and someone said, "Dear Lord, we thank you for being with our friend as she goes through this difficult time, and we are here, gathered in your name, to pray for healing that will allow her to continue on her journey of life and take from this whatever lessons you have in store. We pray this in Jesus' name. Amen." A low chorus echoed, "Amen." The circle remained quiet with heads bowed for several minutes until someone else spoke up to offer a similar prayer. Becky backed away from the bush as soon as she thought no one could hear, shrinking from the voyeurism. She didn't care whether or not Aiyana and Brian stayed, but they followed her.

As they rounded the corner, the prayer stopped, and they heard a small commotion followed by Dmitri's unmistakable voice saying, "I am looking for something."

Becky groaned inside.

"This is a prayer vigil, dude. Can't you look somewhere else?"

They didn't wait to hear the rest of the conversation and hurried toward the lobby entrance, where Kai was waiting. When Dmitri joined them with the device he had retrieved, they decided to go to the coffee house to discuss their findings. Along the way, Becky described to Kai what they had seen.

"Why were they sitting on the ground?" Kai asked. Becky thought it an odd question when there were so many less practical things to wonder.

"The coma," Dmitri said. It took Becky a minute to realize that he was talking about the article in the newspaper two weeks before.

Kai said, "Yeah, I already figured they were there for the kid in the car crash. I meant why weren't they in her room?"

"They were probably under her window," Aiyana said. "Access to the intensive care unit is restricted, and the waiting room is still full of family."

Inside the coffee shop, they claimed a small metal table in the corner and scraped several chairs over to it. Brian had been quiet on the walk over, and Becky noticed he was studying Aiyana. He said, "You didn't think to mention this when we decided to set up the EMF meters at the medical center?"

Aiyana was reading the chalkboard with the brightly colored daily menu. "It's a hospital; everyone has family there. What difference does it make?"

Family makes all the difference, Becky thought.

"Something spiked the meter," Brian said.

Aiyana raised her eyebrows. "Yes, the group of people sitting right next to the device."

"So a person *can* affect the electromagnetic field?" Becky asked.

"Yes," Aiyana said.

"No," Dmitri said at the same time.

"Yes," Aiyana repeated. "Our nerves and muscles operate by electrical signals, so each person has a bioelectric field. Since sodium, potassium, and calcium ions are constantly flowing in and out of cells, the bioelectric field is constantly changing. A changing electrical field creates a magnetic field. Voila, bioelectromagnetism."

"No," Dmitri repeated. "Is negligible, this bio field."

Becky turned to Brian. She couldn't tell anyone, but she desperately wanted to validate the auras that she alone could see. He said, "Well, the instruments are sensitive, so they could pick up on the human effect, but like I said, it should be just background noise. The random presence of people shouldn't make a noticeable spike, unless their fields were somehow aligned...and *moving*."

Dmitri shrugged.

"Well, we saw them, and they were sitting," Aiyana said in a tone that conveyed the matter was closed.

They all got up to place their orders. Becky pulled Brian aside and whispered, "They were *praying*. Doesn't that make a difference?"

He paused, and then nodded. "I think so."

"When two or more are gathered in His name, God will be there," Becky quoted.

The next morning, Dmitri sent a text message: *The coma has ended.*

Later, in the student lounge, Becky recoiled from Aiyana's screaming laughter at her teammates. "Prove the existence of God? You guys are nuts!"

"Shhh," Brian said.

"There's an open meeting room across the hall." Kai tilted his head toward the exit. "Let's go there."

They ushered Aiyana out the door. Her derisive cackling was making even more of a scene than usual of their motley crew, despite the fact that Dmitri's cape was mercifully inconspicuous tucked inside his duffel bag. His t-shirt read: *As a scientist, I am amused by your faith in God. As a theologian, I am amused by your faith in science.*

They retreated across the hall while the other students stared after them. Dmitri brought up the rear of the line, the back of his shirt in full view of anyone watching: *As God, I am amused by your limited world view.* They shut themselves into the meeting room, and once Aiyana stopped laughing, Becky asked, "Don't you believe in God?"

"It's immaterial what I believe. Proving he—or she—exists doesn't solve any problems. In fact, it would raise more questions, such as why are there problems in the first place?" Before Becky could answer, Aiyana turned to Brian. "Surely, you're not serious about wanting to do this."

"I'm not saying we're going to prove the existence of God. I'm saying maybe we could prove the power of prayer. You have to admit that it's an interesting test of Einstein's action at a distance observations."

"Action at a distance?" Becky asked.

Brian said, "Atoms can have an effect on other atoms as far as a building away. Einstein saw it in his data, but he couldn't explain it."

Becky felt excitement stir inside her.

Aiyana broke in. "Big deal, so this girl woke up from her coma. Who's to say prayer did it for her? They've been praying for her since Sunday, so why didn't it happen Thursday instead of Friday? Or Monday instead of Friday, for that matter. Why did it take all week?"

"God works in mysterious ways. They are not for us to know," Becky said.

Aiyana held up a hand in dismissal. "Spare us the platitudes." She didn't slap Becky, but she might as well have.

"Aiyana," Kai said, "I agree that we should do what we decided and be done, but you don't have to be a bitch about it." Becky winced at his comment.

Brian said, "Cool down, people, we're just having a discussion here."

"Fine," Aiyana said, ignoring Becky, who had folded her hands in her lap and was staring straight ahead, trying not to cry. "Say we measure people in prayer groups and churches or whatever, and the electromagnetic field around them spikes when they pray. Then say the guy they pray for gets better, eventually. What does that prove? We have no control situation to compare it to, and there is no way to link cause and effect. He might have recovered in any case. The EM field could just be showing that people feel better about *themselves* when they pray. So let's stick to the original plan."

"We have unexplained data," Dmitri said.

"Welcome to science," Aiyana said. There was a collective hush. Dmitri raised an eyebrow, as though Aiyana were the fool, the newbie, the freshman. "Excuse me," she responded, "sorry to forget for one minute what a genius you are. You contribute so little, it's hard to remember." She launched ahead before he began to speak. "Tell us whatever you're going to tell us without that phony accent. You've been in America for more than half your life. Get over it."

Anyone else would have spit out a retort, but Dmitri did not. Aiyana's words fell into a void like the middle finger in a traffic jam. He turned his back, implying that she wasn't worth the effort. Becky watched Aiyana's emerald green brilliance become muted and muddy.

Dmitri said to Brian, in an accent thicker than ever, "Human electromagnetic field should not have external impact. Human body is conductor. It aligns to stronger field around it. Measure should be negligible."

"Yet after the peak in the field, the energy doesn't return to normal; it dips lower. It's like they were hyper-energized then depleted." Brian showed them the graph again.

"What, you're saying God was there, and then he was gone? Elvis has left the building?" Aiyana scoffed.

Or, Becky thought, prayer is a package of energy sent from us to a loved one.

"This is unexplained data," Dmitri repeated.

Brian rubbed his forehead. "Until we figure out this artifact, we can't even finish the original project, let alone a more provocative one."

Aiyana crossed her arms and drew her right leg over her lap. "This prayer concept is clouding everyone's judgment, like religion always does. We need to find a group of people excited about something completely non-god-related. If their data spikes, too, then it will take prayer off the table so we can move forward."

"How about a study group?" Becky suggested.

Kai said, "Lots of praying will be going on there; mid-terms are coming up." His joke was a welcome crack in the ice. Even Aiyana loosened her posture and shook her head at the ceiling.

"What about a football game?" Kai said. Inside herself, Becky applauded him for contributing.

Dmitri's and Aiyana's expressions were blank, but Brian stood up and clapped Kai on the back. "Of course! Everyone who's been to a good rivalry has felt the energy of the crowd. We can measure it next weekend if we drive over to Missouri for the Kansas-Mizzou game."

"This is not physics energy," Dmitri said.

"Examine your assumptions there, Dmitri." Brian practically bounced around the room. "One person's biofield will align to the earth because the earth's fields are stronger than any individual, but maybe when there are many individuals together with heightened biological activity, they can generate an aggregate field intense enough to show up on the magnetometer. Becky mentioned this to me days ago, but I'm just now catching up." He winked. Becky thought if anyone else could see like she could, her bright pink aura would expose her heart.

Aiyana perked up. "Okay, now we're getting somewhere. We need to establish a baseline with no people around. We can measure ourselves, and if we detect individual readings above the baseline, we'll document the magnitude of variation among us."

Dmitri said, "Random variation will cancel in group readings."

"What do you mean?" Becky dared to ask.

"Have you ever watched little waves coming in at the ocean?" Brian said. "They collide with the water going out from the shore and end up swirling aimlessly like the sand underneath. That's what random variation does; it cancels itself out."

Becky simply nodded because she didn't want to admit that she had never seen the ocean.

"We're testing whether the energy becomes aligned when attention is directed at something, like a big football game or a prayer group. If so, it could add up to a ten-foot wave far bigger than the random swirl around it. That's what should show up on the meter."

Aiyana corrected Brian. "*Could* show up on the meter. We have to get a quiet baseline first of all. We need to go someplace with few manmade interruptions—meaning no phones." She aimed her point at Kai, who shrugged and kept texting.

8

March 1: 55%

Our confrontation over Brian's letter was postponed when Aiyana and Becky decided to finish their trip in the morning. They had moved only twenty miles in two hours, thanks to a traffic accident blocking the road. Becky had long since figured out they were on their way to Brian's lab at New Tech, but she didn't yet know why.

They exited the highway and tried to follow the GPS navigator to the nearest motel, but road construction sent them on a circuitous detour around the neighborhood. Each time they made a mandated turn, the GPS said, "Recalculating."

"Recalculating."

"Recalculating."

"Recalculating."

Becky dialed down the volume. "Why is it that the machine's tone is exactly the same, but it still sounds like she's getting annoyed?"

"I don't know, but I'm about to pitch her out the window," Aiyana said.

At last, the motel lights came into view, and Aiyana veered off to the parking lot. They checked into a room, but Becky wasn't tired, so she rummaged through the drawers: checkout information, Gideon Bible, and area maps. While Aiyana was brushing her teeth, Becky asked, "When we met, did you think we'd ever end up on *two* road trips together?"

Aiyana spat out her toothpaste. "Hell, no."

Becky flipped through the directions to the nearest nature trails, and she said with her beautiful laugh, "I thought you were going to strangle Dmitri on the last one."

"So did I."

9

Siderophobia: Fear of stars

All Aiyana had said was that they needed to find an area with low interference for their baseline test. Becky chirped "camping", and suddenly they were loaded with backpacks full of crap, facing two long nights sleeping on rocks.

Aiyana was in marathon shape and she enjoyed nature—which was a wonder, considering her mother's insistence that she appreciate her heritage by being dragged through the woods around the Great Lakes and every inch of their own reservation—but even she was ready to find a spot and sit down. They had been hiking for three hours over the canyon sides and prairie, around the lake, and through the cottonwood bottomlands. Becky had dropped back to make sure Dmitri Lardass didn't have a heart attack or die from fresh air overexposure or nuclear deprivation or agrizoophobia. Kai and Brian had some bro-mance going on and were racing between the yucca clumps. It was like going on a class trip with a couple of puppies.

"Does anyone actually know where we are?" she asked. No one heard. She stepped off the trail and waited for Becky and Dmitri to catch up, and then asked the question again.

Becky answered, "The website said this is a fishing lake and wildlife preservation area."

"No kidding," Aiyana said, "but where is the camping?"

Becky unfolded a map. "Well, camping is kind of wherever, but the next fire pit is supposed to be…" She rotated the paper clockwise. "Close." In a few more minutes, they came to a metal fire ring with a grill and a spectacular view of the lake.

Dmitri dropped his pack and collapsed onto the ground. Sweat rolled across his flush-red forehead, and his hair was drenched, as were the armpits of his t-shirt. Aiyana was disgusted by the sight.

"Don't get bit by a rattlesnake," Brian said. He and Kai were contemplating a pile of metal poles and canvas. Aiyana could hear Becky next to her take in a breath and hold it, shift her weight, then let her breath out, and repeat. She recognized the telltale indecisiveness as one of the girl's many annoying habits. "If you have something to say to them, spit it out already."

Becky stumbled forward as though Aiyana had pushed her. "Um, guys?" Brian and Kai turned to face her. "Maybe if you…" Becky picked up two poles seemingly at random and fitted them together. She pulled at a ring on the edge of the canvas and pushed it daintily but firmly into the ground. Then she stepped back. Aiyana wished Becky would finish the job, but some antiquity in the girl's thought process made her loathe to bruise fragile male egos.

Kai plopped down at the picnic table, apparently bruised anyway, but Brian said, "Oh, I get it," and went to work setting up the rest of the tent. When he was done, they arranged their equipment inside. They had only been able to scrounge up one tent on short notice, and they agreed it should be used to protect the equipment, in case the weather forecast was wrong and it rained. So the five would be sleeping outside for the next two nights. Aiyana expected the most unpleasant weekend of her life, but she would tough out anything that could get her through graduation with honors.

They piled their sleeping bag rolls in a corner of the tent and gathered around the table. Brian picked up a stick, and in the dirt, he drew a circle intersected evenly by five lines. He wrote one set of initials next to each of the lines. "Okay," he said, assuming the leadership role again. "Let's go find a place to set up these bad boys." He handed three of the magnetometers to Aiyana and pointed to the line next to her initials. "You'll go southwest and set up a triangle, fifty feet on each side. Try to hide the video camera but somewhere you can see most of the enclosed area."

Aiyana grabbed the devices. They had already been over the instructions; she wasn't a child who needed twelve reminders. She wasn't Becky. Graduation, honors, graduation, honors, she repeated in her mind to keep from saying anything out loud.

Brian doled out the remaining equipment and reiterated the other coordinates. "Dmitri, you can set them up here, around the camp, as a control." Dmitri, still lying on the ground, nodded.

They set off with their compasses and measuring tapes to place the devices before dark. Then they would wait. After two nights, they would drive back to school, plug in again, and discover what they had captured. Brian had suggested adding surveillance cameras and factoring them in as a constant because Becky thought the marsh birds and animals might affect the magnetometer readings. Dmitri had answered with his usual "is negligible", but they borrowed the cameras anyway, to capture any human intrusion. Aiyana thought the likelihood of human intrusion was also "negligible"; they had hiked the last hour and a half without encountering a single other soul.

Aiyana tucked one of the devices beneath a yucca plant. She paced off the edges of the triangle where she would set up the rest. The plan was for each of the team members to measure themselves in their assigned fields for two hours at two different times during each day to establish individual baselines. What they would do in the remaining twenty hours weighed heavily on Aiyana's mind. She couldn't bring anything electronic, and she had limited the print books she carried while hiking, but she certainly didn't intend to talk to people to pass the time. Or, heaven forbid, sing campfire songs and roast marshmallows.

She had trouble setting up the camera on the uneven ground behind a sumac bush, so by the time she returned to the campsite Dmitri had already built a fire. He was leaning back against a log, chewing on a piece of beef jerky and tipping up a plastic jug to his lips. He handed the jug to Brian, who sniffed it.

"Ugh, what is that?"

"Russian moonshine."

That was why he struggled on the hike from the car! Well, maybe it would help curb the chill, Aiyana thought. She grabbed the jug and took a swig. Lord, how awful! She spat it out. Dmitri, proud of himself, leaned farther back against his rolled-up sleeping bag and put his feet on the ring around the fire pit. He looked so much like a panda bear lounging after a big meal that Aiyana let out a snort.

She heard Becky behind her start to giggle then draw in a breath. "Dmitri, you're on fire!" Indeed, the edge of his cape had dropped into the pit and was glowing of its own accord. He flapped at it and jumped up, swirling the other edge of his cape through the flames.

"Watch out!" Kai pushed him down and stamped on his cloak. Aiyana had wanted to do that for a long time. "Geez, man!" He laughed with relief. "Maybe you should put that thing in the tent." Kai pointed to the charred purple mess. Dmitri didn't argue.

While Dmitri was in the tent, the others passed around the moonshine. Even Becky took a sip, much to Aiyana's surprise. She choked on it, but still. When Dmitri came back out, Aiyana read his t-shirt: *Mediocrity = The American Dream*. Although she had often thought the same to herself, she hated to see the criticism broadcast on such a smarter-than-thou pig.

"What the heck is your cape made of, anyway?" Kai asked. "I swear it was melting."

"Spray copper and nickel lining. Magnetic shield."

No one knew what to say.

While the others roasted their hot dogs as if they passed for food, Aiyana ate a bean sandwich and an apple. She should have brought something hot and a pair of gloves. She rubbed her hands together and stamped her feet.

After a half hour of blissful quiet around the crack-pop of the campfire, Brian suggested some good old-fashioned ghost stories. It was inevitable that someone would bring it up, but Aiyana had assumed Becky would be the one.

Aiyana also did not expect Kai's response. "I've got one," he said. "My brother told me this when I was a kid, and it scared the piss out of me." Becky leaned forward and fixed her eyes on him. She looked scared already. He started, "Okay, there were these woods, and a girl—" He noticed Becky staring, and he took a deep breath. "There was a girl..." He tilted his head back as if he could read the story written in the sky. "They were in the woods...Um..." His gaze fell back to Becky, and no more words came out.

Aiyana said, "Yeah, Kai, I'm peeing over here. Thanks for the scare." Brian kicked her foot.

Dmitri stood up and said, "I have story. From my homeland." The fire cast a large shadow that extended behind him into the bushes. Aiyana was surprised to feel a shiver as he began to speak. His voice transformed into an echo of the storyteller from his childhood. "On a night like this, a man walked the road and met an old friend. They talked of mountains they climbed and larks of their youth then went to the pub for a toast. The villagers were nicer than ever they were before, and the two reminisced of old things until night reached its darkest and the pub closed down. The friend invited him to join another adventure, and the man was tempted. He missed the times they had, but his life was waiting for him in the morning. So instead, they rode together back toward town, side by side, arriving at daybreak. It was then the man realized he was riding, not on a horse, but a gravestone. His friend had died ten years before, frozen on Lenin Peak. The end."

The story stuck in Aiyana's mind hours later when she was shivering in her sleeping bag next to the dying campfire. Every once in a while, she felt a pellet of rain and heard a sizzle on the embers. Nearby, Becky was trying to curl herself into a tighter ball. It wasn't going to help, Aiyana thought. The human body can only generate so much heat.

Through a gust of wind, she heard the boys talking on the other side of the fire. "We should go into the tent. We'd have to pack like sardines, but at least we'd be warmer."

Kai's voice answered, "Sure, Brian, and you'll be inviting Aiyana? Good luck."

Apparently, Kai was smarter than he let on. Aiyana would freeze solid before she slept within five feet of Dmitri.

Becky whispered, "Maybe we should do what they said. I can't stop shivering."

"Becky, between your crush on Brian, Dmitri's crush on you, and Kai's inclination toward any female that moves, the four of you in a tent together is a recipe for bedlam. No pun intended."

"Shhh…I don't…I wouldn't…You're crazy," Becky said.

Aiyana turned over and tried to sleep.

In the coldest part of the dawn, they rose and built a new campfire. It helped warm their fingers and toes, but it did nothing for Aiyana's or anyone else's disposition. They spent the day avoiding each other, completing their tasks for the research then reading or walking or sitting quietly by the fire.

Late in the afternoon, Becky ended up alone with Kai after she had gone searching for kindling and returned to find him by himself at the camp. He still made her slightly uncomfortable, but she didn't want to be rude, so she tossed the kindling in a pile next to the tent and sat at the picnic table opposite him. He was staring off at the lake. They didn't speak for a minute, and Becky considered leaving, but then she said, "I guess you miss your phone, huh?" She expected a shrug, which would be her cue to get up and go, but to her surprise he answered.

"It's my ticket," he said.

"To where?" she asked.

He focused on a line of ants crawling down the center of the table. He piled several small rocks in front of them, and he and Becky watched while some marched around and some crawled over the top. "People think because I'm 'Asian' or whatever that I'm supposed to like school, but I really don't." He flicked the rocks one-by-one across the campsite. "That kind of sucked when I was a kid who needed help and no one saw me, but oh well, c'est la vie." His cavalier attitude was unconvincing, and Becky wondered how much more of his usual personality was really a poorly fitted mask. "Anyway, I'm hanging on until graduation, when I'll finally have the all-important degree and can commit a hundred percent to my business."

"You have a business?" she asked, unable to hide her surprise.

"Not yet, but I'm building capital with investments. You have to read a lot to keep on top of it. Otherwise, you can lose your money in a hurry."

Becky had never had any money to speak of, but she knew about losing something in a moment. Kai's shallow aura, usually brownish, had turned a brighter orange, betraying his vulnerability. She regretted her assumptions about him. To her, the concept of doing business felt dirty, even though she knew it was necessary. She assumed anyone who did it was selling out, making money from something no one else understood or wanted to touch. It hadn't occurred to her that people might work at business and enjoy it. "I could stay in school forever," she said. "Honestly, I'm afraid of the real world."

He caught her eye, and she couldn't look away. "You don't give yourself enough credit," he said. A shiver ran through her, and it wasn't from the weather. She shook off the feeling. He was only being nice. "You'll have the world wrapped around you, trust me." He got up from the table. "Just don't get caught up in it."

That was the sweetest advice anyone had ever given her.

By the time they gathered around the campfire that evening, no one was eager for another cold night, especially not Aiyana. "Where's that swill you brought, Dmitri?" He passed her the jug, and she choked down a mouthful then rolled the container to Brian. The alcohol burned through her stomach and warmed her to the toes.

Dmitri hadn't changed his t-shirt from the night before, and Aiyana contemplated it through the flickering campfire.

Mediocrity = The American Dream. She heard herself asking, "Why did you come to New Tech, anyway?"

Dmitri answered, "I live here."

When he didn't offer any further explanation, Aiyana clarified. "But you didn't have to go to a state school. Someone like you could have had a free ride with room and board anywhere."

"But I live here."

Okay, Dmitri genuinely did not understand the question. Aiyana had assumed kids in orphanages and foster care didn't consider anyplace home, but who knows what kind of messed up logic was in Dmitri's head. She turned to Becky. "Why did you come?"

Becky drew an arc in the dirt with the toe of her sneaker, and Aiyana thought she might not answer. Finally, she said, "My mom used to tell me that I could make my dreams come true if I picked ones the right size. So I always thought small. Until one of my teachers mentioned a scholarship for this new school in Kansas, and I felt like God was telling me to find a bigger dream."

They were the most words Aiyana had ever heard Becky string together out loud. Honestly, though—God spoke to her? Aiyana surveyed the five of them sitting in the dirt, freezing their butts off, anticipating another night of peeing in the woods. "How's that bigger dream workin' out?"

Brian chuckled and poked a stick in the fire. Becky watched him and started to smile. "Pretty good, I'd say."

Aiyana wanted to puke. "Richter, what about you?" She kicked a rock at Brian.

"New Tech is the most innovative college in the country. Where else would we have to do a real world project to graduate? I mean, Harvard is old school, and MIT and Caltech have their merits, but New Tech is the future of education."

"Put this kid on a brochure," Kai said.

"All right, then, why did you come, Kai?" Brian asked.

"I didn't get into Harvard or MIT. I guess New Tech hadn't filled their quota yet, so here I am. The fact that it has no prestige pissed off my parents, which was a bonus, and it's far enough way that I haven't had to deal with them since."

Aiyana had never heard so many words from Kai, either. Must have been the liquor. The jug came back around to her, and she took another swig.

"Aiyana, what's your excuse?" Kai asked.

"It was the best school I could pay for without applying for scholarships."

She thought Becky's eyes would pop out of her skull. "But you could have gotten money to go anywhere you wanted."

"Why? Because I'm a *minority*?" Aiyana put a sneer on the last word. "No, thanks. I know what everyone is thinking, but I didn't ask for anyone's charity. I can make it on my own merit."

An awkward silence followed, and a log popped in the fire. Becky bowed her head as she said quietly, "I just meant you were smart, that's all."

Aiyana's irritation intensified.

Brian said, "You assume you know what people think, but what do you actually know?"

"Fine, then, what do they *really* think?"

He said, "Anyone who has ever been in a class with you probably thinks the same thing I did, which is that New Tech begged you to enroll."

"That's easy for you to believe; you don't have to deal with the looks."

"I get plenty of looks, thank you very much." At Brian's impish grin, Aiyana's resentment began to subside. "The first blip that crosses a person's mind doesn't count, anyway. Who knows what could have primed it? The intentional thought that comes after is the one that matters. Plus, you're hard to look away from, if you know what I mean."

Aiyana kicked another rock at him.

Kai said, "You wanna know what I think?" She didn't, but he told her anyway. "So what if people pay attention to you because you're hot or smart or they think you're the world's biggest mooch. At least they see you."

The circle fell silent, uncomfortable in neither agreement nor disagreement. A chill wind blew sparks into the air, where they flickered then disappeared.

Eventually, Brian said, "I guess people see what we want them to see." After a moment, he continued. "My folks broke up when I was twelve, and I had no idea. We went to the Natural History museum that day. I knew it was weird because it was a random Thursday and they took us out of school. They made me skip a Little League game, too. That ticked me off. I thought it was the worst thing they could do to me." The other four watched him with curiosity as he spoke into the fire. "I wised up pretty quick when they told us about the divorce—over ice cream, for Pete's sake. It was bad enough to miss baseball, but they ruined mint chocolate chip forever." He lifted his head and flashed his signature smile. The rest of the team mirrored him, because they it was what he wanted. "Then we hit some kid's dog on the drive home."

Becky gasped. Brian huffed at the absurdity of it. "Probably the last emotion my parents shared was the dread of carrying that dog up to the owner's house. What I remember most clearly about the whole day was bonding with the kid through the back windshield, him with his dying dog and me with my dying family. Neither one of us saw it coming."

10

March 2: 54%

I don't know who was more anxious on the way to Brian's lab—Aiyana with her righteous indignation or Becky with the lingering feelings she wouldn't admit. Either way, they were checked out of the motel by eight o'clock in the morning.

Aiyana's indignation was based on a legitimate question: How could Brian live with himself, knowing lives were in danger while he hid in his lab, doing nothing? I had asked myself a similar question many times in recent days.

When they arrived on campus, what Becky saw were the same old memories: an innocent hug and brushing hands here, a heartbreak over there, and beyond, the lab that part of her heart still beat within. Aiyana saw reflections of herself: students bright with possibilities, concerned only about the next exam. That goal to graduate, a desperate need to cross the finish line, was the one thing the two of them shared back then. They didn't yet know the cruel reality: there will always be another exam, another evaluation of your worth to the world. Aiyana had traded her integrity for a piece of paper that meant less and less each passing year.

Students still walked on the opposite side of the street from the theater with its flickering lights misconstrued as ghosts. When New Tech had moved in, the last vestige of the town center with its crumpling interior and faulty wiring was preserved inside a veneer of clean, sharp architecture.

In the Earth and Atmospheric Science building, Aiyana and Becky passed through a security gate, a new addition and another reminder that we were no longer quite welcome in a place that had once been home. As they climbed the metal staircase to Brian's third floor lab, Aiyana was ticking off the many ways she would take the poor bastard to task. She didn't realize at the point how much he had changed.

When he came out of his office, I know what she saw because I had seen it, too. His demeanor overshadowed any expression on his face. All of the annoying charm and nauseating qualities of joy and optimism had disappeared. The charisma lingered, but it was dim. The remainder was a hollow intensity, like a black hole, its gravity pulling together what was left of Brian.

Aiyana couldn't bring herself to say any of the things she had planned during the night. Piling on her accusations would have been like dropping a stone on a heap of rust.

"Aiyana," he said.

"Brian," she said.

They were no longer friends but not quite strangers, trying to pretend that they had parted under better circumstances, unable to forget the past full of guilt and fear and mutual disrespect.

11

Sophophobia: Fear of learning new things

As the team cleaned up the campsite to prepare for their return, Becky watched the smoke tendrils curl up from the extinguished flames. Brian brushed his hands together to rid them of the ashes and bumped his shoulder to hers. "Whatcha thinkin'?"

She said, "Do you know the saying, 'where there's smoke, there's fire'? It isn't true, is it?"

"Why not?"

"Well, after the fire goes out, there's smoke. If people followed the smoke, they'd only find where a fire *had* been. They'd be too late."

"I suppose you're right." He put a brotherly arm around her. "We've probably learned a lot of things that will turn out not to be true."

During their return hike, the cold front from the night before clashed with the sun breaking through the clouds, and lightning flashed in the distance. They continued walking as fast as they could to try to reach their car before the storm reached them. A crack of thunder, loud and close, made them duck; then they scrambled along the trail, attempting to outrun the inevitable. The clouds opened and poured out the rain, and with nowhere to go for shelter, they stopped in the middle of a creek bridge and laughed. After a few minutes, the sun won out and a rainbow appeared over the water. Becky breathed in the fresh after-aroma of the shower and marveled aloud about negative ions, nature's waste removal. Aiyana said most of the scent was actually bacteria released from the soil during the rain. Either way, they agreed it smelled good.

When they arrived back on campus, they headed straight for the student center, so anxious to see the data that they didn't stop to change their damp clothes. The team waited with their computers while Brian hooked up the first device. The rest of the devices were spread out on the conference table in the meeting room they had reserved for the afternoon, and the camping equipment was piled in a corner.

Brian extracted the files then sent them to Becky. She immediately began to load them into the database, determined to keep up. It was fun to search for surprises in the results, but soon the numbers began to blur together. Certainly nothing but a computer algorithm could recognize a pattern in so much data. As soon as she was done, Dmitri would run the algorithms he and Brian had designed. Dmitri was seated on the floor with his cape spread beneath him like a picnic blanket. Becky resolved to take the thing to the cleaners, whether he agreed or not.

Kai was skimming the three days of videos to check for any human interference. It was something he could do with minimal attention span, which apparently suited him fine. Becky thought of what he had told her and how opposite they were in their views on school. She sat in front during every lecture and studied her notes as soon as she got home. She was a fixture at office hours and tutorials.

Her little rural high school had taught her a lot, but when she reached college, she wished she had learned more. After three years of catch-up, she still didn't trust her instincts for making connections in her studies, although she found that many of the insights other students voiced were ones she had thought to herself. It was a relief to know she deserved to be admitted, and she should have been content with that. But deep down, she wasn't. She didn't want her thoughts to be commonplace. Deep down, she both admired and envied Aiyana, who was the antithesis of ordinary.

One of Aiyana's roles on the project was to sort through previous research on directed energy and other published papers related to the project. There was so much information on the Internet that Becky didn't know what was significant or true, but Aiyana had no problem classifying ideas into gold versus bunk. In general, "bunk" included both of the things Becky believed in with all her heart: God and her special sight. However, Aiyana appeared to know what she was doing, and she was certainly confident about it.

"Last one," Brian announced, and a few seconds later, the beep sounded on Becky's computer, alerting her to a new file in her inbox. She finished the spreadsheet she was working on and clicked the upload button then sent a notice to Dmitri.

"Next to the last one!" she said. Dmitri barely grunted when his laptop sounded its tone.

A few minutes later, Kai lowered the lid of his computer. "Nothing here but a couple of bunny rabbits." He winked at Becky and passed her a note with a string of numbers: 2:40, 3:23, 5:55, etc. What was that all about? But he had already left the room. Probably went to study up on his investments, she thought.

The excitement in Brian's voice broke through her curiosity. "Hey guys, look at this!" She shoved the note from Kai into the pocket of her jeans and pulled the bottom cuff of her sweatshirt down to her knees. Dmitri projected the line graphs from his computer screen onto the wall. Brian touched the wall with his finger, circling five points on the graph, where there were increasingly high peaks in the data. "This is from one triangle set. The other sets were pretty well flat, but this group shows these weird spikes, as though something passed through the field, each time with bigger and bigger energy. It looks like it stayed nearby, too, because the energy level never returns to baseline." Brian scanned the room. "Where is Kai? Didn't he say there was nothing in the videos?" He seemed annoyed.

"I'm sure he'll be back in a minute," Becky said, to no real effect. She was staring hard at the graph. "Dmitri, what are those numbers on the bottom?"

"That is the x axis," he said.

Well, she knew that. His condescension made her feel ashamed, but she tried on a little of Aiyana's confidence and said, "Yes, but are those time measurements?"

"They are time coordinates by fifteen-minutes. Twelve o'clock, twelve-fifteen, twelve-thirty, twelve—"

"Okay, thanks." She cut him off and fished in her pocket for the paper Kai had given her. She read the first number on the list: *2:40*. She looked back at the graph. There was a spike just before two forty-five. *3:23*. A bigger spike before three thirty. *5:55*. Yes, the largest spike occurred at six AM. The rest of the times in Kai's note also corresponded to peaks on the graph. "Guys?" she said.

No one was paying attention to her. Brian and Dmitri were arguing over what the graphs might mean, and Aiyana was cursing an absent Kai for being such a lazy ass that they had to review the videos again. Becky lifted the lid of the computer Kai had left on the table. The screen flickered on, and the relevant video was still open. She scrolled to the 2:40 time point and saw a rabbit's nose come into focus in the dark, sniffing the camera; then the animal bounded away. She started to laugh to herself. At 3:23, the glowing gray form of another rabbit entered the field of vision. It sniffed the air and cautiously approached the camera but turned away before reaching it. A third rabbit entered the clearing as the sky began to lighten. It stopped short at the edge of the field and ran away. Becky laughed to herself and said quietly, "It was the bunnies!" Then a bobcat shot across the field.

She didn't have a chance to tell the others because suddenly the fire alarm sounded, and Kai burst through the door. "Someone found a bomb!" Uncomprehending, they stared at him while the alarm screeched, paralyzing their consciousness. He grabbed his computer and Becky's and pulled her by the sweatshirt toward the door. "We have to get out of the building!"

The rest scrambled to gather up the computers that held their all-important data, leaving their sleeping bags, backpacks, and magnetometers in the room.

12

Astynomiaphobia: Fear of police

Outside the student center, the five team members watched the police cars and lights surround the quad. Among the many other students evacuated from the building and the growing numbers of spectators, Aiyana was acutely aware that she hadn't washed properly in three days. She was about to suggest to Brian that they all go back to their rooms and read about the bomb online when the campus police exited the building. Her curiosity held her tongue.

The policemen turned their focus on the teammates—they were no doubt a sight—and conferred with each other. Surely it's not a crime to be unkempt, Aiyana thought. Otherwise, Dmitri would be on the Most Wanted list. One of the policemen walked in their direction, and upon reaching them, said, "Would the five of you come with me, please?" Another police officer appeared to herd them back into the building.

Aiyana could sense that Brian and the rest were as bewildered as she was. The other students were staring. Aiyana was used to attracting looks, and she was generally aware but able to ignore it. She hadn't considered how benign the attention had been at the root: furtive glances born of insecurity around the unfamiliar, and jealousy grown from begrudging admiration. She thought she had perceived judgment in the stares before, but that was a figment in a cloud compared to the verdicts pressing in now, causing her skin to tighten like a shield. Nothing she had personally experienced had ever been so palpable. Accusatory whispers stung like pellets of hail as the police officers paraded the teammates across the quad.

Growing up on the periphery of prejudice against her father, she had believed she shared in his injustice. But only at that moment did she begin to understand what he had experienced. She recalled a framed verse in her parents' living room—something about peace, patience, kindness, goodness, gentleness, and self-control. Her father embodied that fruit of the spirit, overcoming indignation every day of his young adult life. Admiration welled up inside her for the strength and work it must have taken for him to become such a gracious man.

She also felt a new compassion for Dmitri, who had revealed around the campfire bits and pieces from his childhood at the orphanage after his father was convicted. The attention he drew must have felt like pellets also, and magnified to an eight-year-old because kids don't have the decency to keep their suspicions to a whisper. Dmitri's shield was the cape his father had given him, which the sisters had mended time and again until Dmitri had no choice but to buy a new one.

Between two police officers, Dmitri walked across the quad with his head held high and his t-shirt proudly shouting:

If stupidity fell like apples, I'd never go hungry around here. Only a few hours before, Aiyana had secretly laughed at it, identifying with the sentiment. But Dmitri's arrogance was public, attracting daggers like a high-powered magnet. Her compassion turned to visceral hatred.

After two hours of questioning at the police station about their whereabouts over the past three days, how they had obtained the devices, and what they were using them for, the five teammates were released. The bomb scare had been the result of a dud discovered next to a couch in the student lounge. It was the second left on campus in the past week. The first had been on the quad near the physics building, where a couple of students had reported seeing a guy in a cape prowling the vicinity and other places on campus. They had also provided descriptions of the magnetometers, which had been spotted in the same areas. The police had been trying to reach Dmitri for two days, but of course he hadn't responded and could not be located, which raised suspicions further. So when his student ID showed up in a room full of devices as advanced as military technology, they thought they had the culprit. Fortunately, all five stories about the project matched, and since the team had been in the wilderness together when the first bomb was found, there was no reason to hold them.

Aiyana wasn't entirely comfortable being Dmitri's alibi. The kid was still *off*, no matter how smart he was.

Being tied together with an attempted bombing created more than enough intimacy for all of them, especially after the confessionals around the campfire, so the five agreed to go their separate ways for the night. They would shower, sleep, and meet again in Brian's dorm the next day to continue their data analysis. When they left the police station, Dmitri uttered under his breath, "Nachalstvo," like a dirty word. *Authority*.

The following morning, Aiyana had a renewed urgency to get back on track toward her summa cum laude. As she walked from her dorm in East Campus to Brian's dorm in West Campus, she was at least glad that the other students had short attention spans. They didn't seem to recognize her as the same person ignobly paraded across campus in suspicion of a felony. Rubbernecking males disregarded her face entirely, and sideways glances from females held nothing more than Darwinian rivalry. Classmates she had already outsmarted passed with their usual tight-lipped acknowledgment, and those she hadn't outsmarted yet regarded her skin with curiosity but not recognition. All of their attention was familiar, even if wasn't harmless.

She was the first to arrive at Brian's room. "You're early," he said, stepping into the hall and closing the door behind him. "Let's go to the common room." He scribbled a note to the others and taped it to the door.

"What's the matter, did your roommate finally come out of hiding?"

"Heck, no, he flunked out already! I just haven't picked up since he left."

While they sat on the couches in the common room, waiting for the others, Brian and Aiyana mused about the bombs. "It's funny nobody saw the person who set them.

Makes you wonder how long they'd been there before someone noticed," Brian said.

"Or did something about it. I'll bet more people saw it than reported it."

"Yeah, probably. Do you suppose the guy is trying to send a message by setting duds?"

"You give him too much credit. I think he's just an idiot."

Brian laughed. "Of course you do." He got up and went to the window overlooking the sidewalk. "Speaking of idiots, that was some Russian moonshine Dmitri whipped up, wasn't it?"

It took Aiyana a minute to understand what he was talking about. "I thought we agreed not to dwell on that unfortunate incident."

"I changed my mind. I wanted to mention it before it gets awkward."

Too late, Aiyana thought, as their meeting in the woods two nights before sprung up between them like an inflatable elephant. They had each set off in search of a place to empty themselves of the volumes of alcohol they had consumed in their boredom and cold. They got turned around and stumbled into the same tiny closet of bushes. "I thought you were a rattlesnake!" "I thought you were a lion!" They collapsed together, chortling with abandon, the world glowing silver with moonlight and the haze of intoxication. Then he kissed her. Or she kissed him. They would never know for sure. All Aiyana could remember was that while her lips were on his, she noticed he still smelled clean after two days in the woods, which struck her as funny. He had pulled back, and his confusion made her laugh out loud, which made him laugh, too, until they were both roaring in a way that clarified one thing: if they had been sober, such a thing would not have happened. "We shall never speak of this." "Never."

But Brian had spoken of it. Aiyana sighed. "I know a lot of girls swoon over you…"

"And you are off the charts on the campus hotties list."

"How charming," she said.

"I try." He grinned.

"But I am not attracted to you in the least."

"And my appreciation of your attributes is purely objective. Or objectifying."

She smirked. "So there's no need for this to be awkward."

"None at all."

Aiyana got up from the couch and crossed to the window on the opposite side of the room from Brian. "Plus, there's Becky to consider."

Brian blinked. "Wait, you and Becky?"

"What? No. I'm talking about her crush on *you*," Aiyana said.

"Oh." Brian narrowed his eyes. "You're saying you *would* want to go out with me except that you're stepping aside for Becky's sake? How unselfish. And so unlike you."

"Don't flatter yourself. What I'm saying is that obviously both of us have gone too long without a date if we're considering each other, even under the influence. So you should give Becky a shot."

"Fair enough. Becky and I can double date with you and Dmitri. He's kinda sweet on you." Brian winked at her.

"You disgust me."

Becky and Kai burst into the common room. "It was the animals," Becky announced.

Then Dmitri arrived, almost on time. Kai opened his computer on a coffee table, and they gathered around it. Becky pointed to the video clips of the rabbits then the bobcat, and showed how the timing lined up exactly with the graph from Dmitri. "Does this ruin our project?" she asked.

"We catch the cat," said Dmitri.

As always, they waited for him to explain. Surely Dmitri was not suggesting the animals were a real world problem to solve, Aiyana thought. If so, she would refuse.

Dmitri started to pace. "We know the energy patterns of a predator stalking prey."

They all still stared at him.

"Do you not see?" Dmitri said. "We can catch the campus bomber. This will be our term project."

Aiyana watched their faces as the team contemplated Dmitri's proposal. They couldn't honestly think his idea was feasible. "Hold on a minute," she said. "We've switched topics twice already, and we have already collected data on something we might actually be able to do." Dmitri didn't argue, which meant his mind was made up and she wasn't worth the airtime. Her blood boiled, and she crossed her arms. "We're not changing mid-stream again. We'd be throwing the project together, and the report wouldn't be worth the paper it was printed on."

"Let's think about this objectively," Brian said. He put a hand on her shoulder, and she jerked away. "We're supposed to solve a real world problem, but what we've been planning is essentially a non-problem. I don't think I'm alone when I say that it has always made me a little uneasy, taking a shortcut like that."

"But you agreed!" Aiyana said.

"Yes, I did, because we didn't have any better ideas. Now we do."

Becky, like an obedient puppy, would do whatever Brian said. Aiyana thought Kai would be on her side, if only to get away with as little work as possible, but he was standing oddly close to Becky. Aiyana was backed into a corner. "No," she said, tightening her arms and steadying her stance.

"Can I talk to you a minute?" Brian said. He gestured her to follow him into the hall. She did, although reluctantly.

"I said no," she repeated.

Brian held up both hands, palms toward her in surrender. "We're not going to force you into a project you don't want to do. We need your input too much. All I ask is for you to think about it. If we measure a football game and find an energy pattern, or if we prove there's no increase in EMF near the physics lab, do you really believe it's going earn you a summa cum laude? And wouldn't you rather do something that matters?"

She hated how well he could read her.

13

March 2: 55%

It was hard to believe nine years could make such a difference. I watched as Brian turned away from Aiyana's shock at his appearance. When his eyes met Becky's, his face changed to that smile she alone could elicit. He enveloped her in a hug, and the schoolgirl blush rose in her cheeks.

"Congratulations!" he said.

Becky pulled back. "For what?" Brian stepped away— awkwardly, of course. He knew about the baby because I had told him. He had been warned to expect our reunion. Becky whirled around toward the back of the lab. "Where is he? What did he say?"

Brian put a hand on her arm then took it away. "Maybe…he should explain."

Aiyana slowly scanned the room, her eyes filled with accusation. I knew then she had figured out how Brian could continue his research for so many years yet publish nothing and say nothing—because I had funded him. Her obvious anger was rooted in self-righteousness, but she also wanted to protect Becky. That was the one important thing we had in common.

Aiyana pushed past Brian and pulled his letter from her purse. She spread the graphs and the bulls-eye map—evidence of our guilt—onto the alchemist table that Brian used for workspace. Then she stood up, put a hand on her hip, and directed her contempt toward the door. "Are you going to tell Becky, or should I?"

14

Phobophobia: Fear of fear

Becky tried to anticipate Aiyana's response at being outnumbered on the decision to change the term project. If Brian could convince her to agree, then Aiyana would probably need to get the upper hand. Her expectations were confirmed when the two returned to the common room, Brian coming in second, and Aiyana said, "Okay, if we're going to catch this guy, we have to move fast. We need a damn clear model of the animal patterns and a hypothesis for what we think we're going to see on campus with all the interference from the cell phones and wi-fi, etcetera. We can use the data we've already collected as a baseline so we don't lose half our work." She obviously felt better taking charge. Becky filed away the insight for future reference.

Brian grinned. "Right on." Then he frowned. "It's too bad we didn't leave any of the devices here while we were gone, or we could have had a head start."

Aiyana waved him off. "That's fine. We're going to need permission from the campus police to leave those things lying around; I don't intend to get hauled in for questioning again.

We'll also need a plan for what to do when we see something. The guy might not be so incompetent the third time."

They set to work mapping out a plan. Their hypothesis assumed the bomber would leave a similar energy pattern as the bobcat stalking rabbits in the wild. Becky would do whatever was asked of her, but something about their hypothesis bothered her. She didn't want to speak up to the team because she didn't have verifiable data, and Dmitri had told her a hundred times that bunnies are negligible, making her feel negligible, too. Still, she thought they were ignoring something important: the bunnies were scared.

When everyone else had gone off to start their assignments, Becky decided to ask Brian to explain the magnetometers again. She said, "Would the measurements look the same if the energy of whatever we measured had been decreasing rather than increasing? Because they're both movement, and movement creates magnetism, right?"

"Yes and no," he said. "The devices measure protons affected by a magnetic field. So when the kinetic energy or motion that created the field decreases, the effect isn't as strong. If the decrease were fast enough, though, I guess it could flip the magnetism in the opposite direction, and that would look the same in the readings. We didn't study the direction of the proton effect, but maybe we should."

"Dmitri thinks the patterns show the bobcat's energy as it's revved up stalking his prey, right? But couldn't some of the effect be the scared rabbits?"

Brian scrunched his eyebrows. "I suppose. The rabbits have a biological response to flee, which might increase their energy output. We'd have to ask Aiyana about it." He shrugged. "If that's what happened, though, there should have been a dip in intensity each time a rabbit exited the measurement area, but there wasn't. So I can't say they had much effect."

Becky knew there was another explanation. Fear left a trace. She could see it, ever since the Christmas Eve she and Mum had spent the day drinking homemade cocoa with cinnamon and making paper chains and popcorn strings to decorate their spruce tree that still smelled fresh from the snow. While they walked to church in the light of the moon, her mother had glowed with love. It was the first time Becky could both feel it and see it. It was the last time her mother would leave the house without checking all of the windows and checking them again, or walk under the eaves without glancing into the shadows, or enter her own home without hesitating.

When they returned from church, the first thing Becky saw was the string of popcorn under the radiator. The second thing she saw was Mum's glow flare a deep red. The third thing she saw was the strange man reaching toward her. Then she sensed his arm around her neck, the salt of his hand across her mouth, the smell of stale cigarettes, the heave of muscle as he shoved her mother to the floor, and the sound of breaking bones.

The moon continued to shine through the open door like it didn't know what was happening. The cold air ventured in and was trapped by the scene while the warm cinnamon escaped into the night.

Helpless on the floor, her mother begged the man to let Becky go. For some reason, he did. She fell against the radiator, and he ran out to the van that they had not seen parked in the shadows.

The stranger was gone, but the fear remained. Over time, Mum's glow faded away, and Becky realized a vital truth: At first, fear stirs you up, but then it sucks the life out of everything around you.

15

Scoptophobia: Fear of being seen

Aiyana had not intended to be back at the campus police station so soon—or ever. Yet a short week later, the five of them were facing a high counter in a row of plastic chairs, next to two students waiting to pay for parking tickets. The desk officer had recognized them all when they walked in, and he told them to "sit tight". Aiyana was about as tight as she could get.

She sneaked a glance at Dmitri from the corner of her eye. He had his feet pulled up in his chair, and his cape was wrapped around him. The toe of one sneaker poked out beneath. Heaven only knew what his t-shirt said because it was mercifully hidden. The other four team members had successfully faded into the background, their ignominy of the previous week already forgotten by the other students on campus. But the attention on Dmitri had increased exponentially, according to Becky, who had walked home with him after their last meeting. The general consensus on campus was that he was the bomber; the police just couldn't prove it yet.

"Okay, what do you kids need?" the officer asked, emerging from a back room.

"We have some data to show you, from readings we were taking when the first bomb was planted," Brian said.

"Let's see it."

Brian's expression said *Here?*, but the policeman made no move toward a more private setting. So Brian opened his laptop and placed it on the high counter. He had to reach up to the keyboard like a little kid. "We found a pattern in the few days prior to when the first bomb was reported. It's almost identical to the pattern with the bobcat, only we didn't see it right away because it was spread over a longer time. We figure it shows the bomber staking out the area. We've looked at the models, and we're pretty confident that we'll see the same thing if he tries it again. We just have to be able to collect the data."

"Bobcat?"

Spurred on by the officer's mild interest, the group explained in a jumble about the rabbits and the camping trip and their strategy for planting magnetometers again and taking real-time readings to share with the police.

"Well, son,"—the policeman spoke to Brian—"interesting stuff, but we can't let you leave strange electronics all over campus. It will scare people and hamper the investigation."

"Yes, why catch real criminals?" Dmitri said under his breath.

"What was that?" the officer said, walking over to stand his full height above Dmitri, who didn't look up. The officer leaned closer to him. "We know who you are, boy. We have our eyes on you." The students in the chairs next to them nudged each other.

"Sir," Brian said politely. "We think we can do it better than before. We can leave the devices sewn into curtains or in the pocket of our jackets on the back of a chair. If we could get permission to do those things, no one would have to notice."

The policeman contemplated the suggestion. He scanned the faces of the team members in turn, landing for a long time on Dmitri. Aiyana wanted to say it would be one way for the cops to keep a closer watch on the weirdo, but she kept quiet. "You all would have to tell us if you see anything."

"Yes, sir," Brian said, barely hiding the excitement in his voice.

"I mean immediately, as soon as you see it. How long does it take to read these things?"

"We think we've figured out a way to sync up wirelessly in near real time, or at least every couple of hours. If not, we can collect the data manually once a day."

"So, once a day. You say this builds up over several days?"

"That's what happened the first time."

"Fine. But don't be conspicuous about it."

Aiyana saw the two students in the waiting area whispering as the team left the station, and Dmitri's cape flapped in the breeze from the door. Inconspicuous was impossible.

16

March 2: 56%

I had rarely seen Becky get angry, but I saw it happen in Brian's office when she realized he and Aiyana knew something she didn't know about her own marriage. I didn't need special vision to sense her head-to-toe glow rolling inward, away from Aiyana and Brian, too. Aiyana tried to protest her innocence, but Becky didn't respond. Not actively, anyway. She withdrew and left the lab. It's a good thing she was so absorbed in her mind, or else she would have noticed me lurking in the hall, waiting for the right time. But she didn't see me. That wasn't unusual in those days.

Aiyana and Brian didn't bother to go after her. Brian's data always came first to him, and Aiyana avoided nurturing whenever possible. I let Becky go, too. After all, how could the person who caused the situation be the one to make her feel better about it?

Instead, I continued as the observer while Brian and Aiyana tried to bridge a gap of nine years. He showed her his binders of envelopes, postmarked and unopened, and pages of charts and graphs stapled with newspaper clippings, printouts from the Internet, and letters from across the country—a timeline of his single-minded life. Vicious crimes of desperation in cities and small towns, furious and destructive suburban mobs—massive acts of senseless violence from sea to shining sea. Few people thought horror could happen in their neighborhoods. Many didn't believe the perpetrators were capable of such things. Most said there were no clear signs. Brian's data said otherwise.

Each section of Brian's binders contained a map and a calendar, covered with clouds of uncertainty that became smaller and smaller as time went on and his precision increased. Then the latest, the cluster at the beginning of June with Freedom, Kansas at the epicenter.

The wooden table was covered in paper, and Aiyana leaned over it, her body blending in so that it seemed the table wasn't holding her up; rather, she was the foundation. Brian reached over Aiyana and inserted into the latest binder a recent printout from the Associated Press about the newsflash she and Becky had heard the day before, the deadly road rage incident in Alum Rock, California. Aiyana read the quote in the box at the bottom of the article: *A person with that much anger shouldn't be allowed to drive.*

The date and location the incident had occurred were squarely within the clouds of Brian's prediction. "A radius of ten miles and one week has been consistent and unimproved for the past year," Brian said as Aiyana pored over the recent pictures and articles. "Apparently we've reached the maximum accuracy possible with current technology."

"How many energy devices are you reading?"

"We're integrated into a navigational app for mobile phones now. Any time the phone is on, readings can be taken automatically and sent back to our database together with the latitude and longitude." His eyes flickered in my direction, but fortunately, Aiyana was distracted by the phone in her hand, no doubt considering the implications of what we were doing. "The app currently has nearly a million users."

Aiyana looked around the lab, such as it was. The cluttered and enclosed space was more like a library in a crazy man's castle. I had told Brian countless times that it did not convey a sense of respect for himself and his work. But he wasn't worried about respect or funding. That was my job. I'm the one who made the industry connections and pitched the phony business plan that got us integrated into the phone application. The investors would get their money; we just couldn't tell them how. Aiyana stood up and crossed her arms. "So, this is basically an outcome model for human behavior, without the user's knowledge."

"Yes and no," Brian answered, noncommittal per usual. "We don't keep identifiers in the data. We aren't tracking individuals." He didn't say why, but we heard it anyway: *We don't want to repeat that mistake.* "We do model *aggregate* energy patterns. As long as the overall energy is steady at any level, or as long as it is increasing and decreasing randomly across an area, people adapt to the environment. However, when a sharp decline in aggregate energy is paired with stagnation in movement, those conditions make it increasingly likely that someone will reach a breaking point. Again, though, the pattern only predicts when and where, not who or what."

She didn't push him further on his model and its intent, which was surprising. Maybe she was going easy because his psyche was near the edge. Instead, she pointed to the unopened envelopes. "Why those? Paper is archaic."

"Oh, tradition, I guess." He shifted uncomfortably. "When I started, I didn't have any way to register my predictions with consistency, so I mailed them to myself, Becky, you, and—well, until the latest."

Brian had used the "tradition" to keep in touch with them all, and Aiyana's tense body said she knew it. She didn't look at him. She probably considered it pathetic, cowardly, and unnecessary—needing people, that is. "I don't read them," she said.

"I know."

There was no avoidance in their confessions; they were as honest as they used to be. Aiyana could have asked a dozen questions: Why had he continued to send the letters to her? How did he know she was going to open the last one? What would he have done if she had never responded? The answer would have rankled her because the truth was that Brian could still read her after so much time; she was predictable. All except her friendship with Becky.

Aiyana turned back to the latest prediction, a cloud of uncertainty around a time period three months away. "We have to protect her," she said. But Brian and I had already hurt Becky time and time again, with her own sympathy, with every envelope full of human suffering. It killed her joy to open those letters. I didn't stop him from sending them, though. I let her hurt. Because I wanted her to know that while the world suffered, her hero Brian was holed up in his office, checking the box to confirm it happened. She believed Brian when he said he couldn't act upon his data. But I could. I built my risk management firm by acting on his predictions. It's easy to manage risk when you know the future, especially when no one else does.

"We have to tell her, " Aiyana said.

Brian sat heavily in a metal chair.

Aiyana's expression refused sympathy. The defeated man slumped on that chair was not the Brian she knew. Not the Brian that Becky loved. Then again, neither was I.

"And we have to tell the police."

His head jerked up in alarm, a wild animal caught in a trap.

17

Symbolophobia: Fear of symbolic ideas

"I'm worried about him," Brian said to Aiyana on their analysis shift one night. The campus rumors about Dmitri had grown while the team focused on lining curtains and planting jackets to collect the data they needed. They decided to review the data in two-hour blocks, driven not only to catch the bomber but also to clear Dmitri's name. "I think this is bringing back everything he went through after his dad was convicted, with people treating him like he was guilty by association."

Aiyana said, "If you're going to act like a freak, you have to expect people will treat you like one."

"He was just a kid."

"He's not a kid any more. Face it, he brings this on himself."

Brian sighed. "Your compassion is inspiring." He typed a note on one of the graphs and flipped to the next day's chart.

"What, you don't think he wears a shiny purple cape to get attention?"

"You know that also started when he was a kid. Becky has an interesting theory about it. She thinks people react coldly to him because the spray metal lining in the cape keeps his own heat from radiating, and his personality was shaped in response to their reaction. Kind of a vicious circle."

"Yeah, yeah, Becky Our Lady of Empathy."

Brian stopped working . "Why are you so hard on her?"

Aiyana continued to mark her spreadsheet for each data angle she had reviewed. *X. X. X.* Nothing. Nothing. Nothing. "She bugs me. The way she's always sweet and demure and innocent, and she's so self-righteous."

"*She's* self-righteous?"

"Yes, her, little Miss Becky. Don't you hear the Christianese she speaks? She thinks she knows about gods and the universe."

"So do you. What's the difference?"

"The difference is that I'm right."

Brian raised his eyebrows, and Aiyana had to smile. It was annoying, the way he made her think in patterns she preferred not to.

She expected Brian to laugh, but his expression was serious. "You think you understand all there is to understand in the world?"

She scowled. "Don't tell me you're a Christian, too. You want to be a scientist!"

"I'm not talking about religion. That's a man-made thing." He held up his computer and turned its layers of graphs toward her. "I'm talking about the stuff I see every day that I can't explain. That science can't explain."

"That doesn't mean you should believe whatever myth exists to explain it and assume its occurrence is a miracle. When the technology improves enough, we'll know the real explanation."

He closed his computer. "So you admit there are things in this world that you don't understand."

"Of course." She set aside her spreadsheet and shifted her full attention to Brian. She didn't like where his head was at. "But it doesn't mean they're incomprehensible. It doesn't prove there is a God."

"Likewise, comprehension doesn't prove there *isn't* a God. The more I learn about science and the laws of physics and the order of the world, the more I'm in awe of the universe."

"So, you're one of those who would find a watch in the woods and assume there was a watchmaker."

"Yes and no." He grabbed a piece of scrap paper. "If I found a watch in the woods, I would assume someone had manipulated nature to put it together in such a complex way. So, a watchmaker, yes. But a watchmaker is not a god. We all can create something out of what we find in nature." As he talked, Brian folded the piece of paper into the shape of a fox. "My mascot," he said as he handed the origami to Aiyana. She rolled her eyes. "Miracles are different," he said. "Miracles are something outside the cosmic order, and any force that can manipulate the cosmos is too big to be human. So, God."

"In short, God is your name for a force we can't see."

"Are there any forces we can see? Gravity, for example?"

"We see it every day when we don't float off to space."

"That's the *effect* of gravity. The force itself is invisible. As Heisenberg said, 'What we observe is not nature itself, but nature exposed to our method of questioning.'"

"You think because you believe in it, you can model the

force of God, but I won't understand because I'm an atheist?"

"No, but existing models leave a lot unexplained, and I think the force of God is somewhere in the void. Heisenberg also said we ask questions about nature in the language we know."

"Exactly," Aiyana said. "We used to think the atom was the smallest piece of matter, but now we can explain atoms in terms of quarks. Quarks, not God. The families that make up the quarks can't be split apart, but just because we don't have the capability to do it yet."

Brian shrugged. "The idea of quark families is a bit of a myth itself, isn't it? We can't split them apart, so we don't actually know what they are." She started to protest, but he stopped her. "Assume for the sake of argument you're right. What you're saying is that nothing will ever be the smallest piece of matter because there could always be better technology in the future to study it."

"Well…" She sensed a trick question. "Yes."

"So, with infinitely advanced technology, you could split the atom and the quark and the family and whatever comes after that, down to the tiniest singularity which is basically nothing. That means the infinity of the universe arose from the infinity of nothingness. Sounds a lot like an argument for Creation."

"Sounds more like an argument for the Big Bang."

"Same thing."

"Your stubbornness is irritating," she said.

"Right back at ya, babe."

18

March 2: 57%

I continued to watch Brian after Aiyana left the lab in search of Becky. He was frantic, pacing, talking to himself. He knew he had to act, but there were so many risks with getting involved.

It was disconcerting to see Brian straighten his papers then put them back in the binders and back on the shelf, as if he were rewinding the night, rearranging time to when he was just a passive observer. But as much as he knew that the past and present are blended more than we think, he also knew that being *just* an observer wasn't possible. Quotes from scientists adorned his wall like artwork and betrayed his inner conflict:

> "Observations not only disturb what is to be measured, they produce it."
>
> – Pascual Jordan

> "Separation of the observer from the phenomenon to be observed is no longer possible."
>
> – Werner Heisenberg

For weeks, I had known we had to do something, ever since I saw the Freedom data. Brian was more scared than reason, and he had been waffling between yes and no ever since. When Becky and I learned we had finally been matched as adoptive parents, I had to force Brian to make a choice—the right choice.

I had never forced him to do anything. Years before, at the beginning of our collaboration, eight people died in a mall shooting within one hundred miles and six months of his prediction, and I was horrified. I wanted to stop the next one before it happened. But Brian said he couldn't model the patterns leading to an event if we were actively trying to change the event. I argued that it didn't matter, that saving lives was more important. He argued that a prediction within a hundred-mile radius and a six-month window was useless. He compared it to landfall predictions for hurricanes, which only protect people when they're accurate, and have only improved because data has been collected and modeled for decades. That wouldn't have been possible if people could simply change the weather when they didn't like the forecast. He convinced me that we could save a thousand times as many lives once we maximized our predictive accuracy, but it meant we had to observe, not intervene, at least for the time being. So I agreed to wait. Year after year. Catastrophe after catastrophe.

The stakes were too high, and too close, to wait any more.

Ironically, the one person who could make him see reason would be Becky, but Brian's lack of intervention didn't bother her. To her, opening each envelope was like watching a sad story on the news; it hurt to know, but the reporter wasn't to blame.

I had never mentioned to her my arrangement with Brian. The secrecy started when my insurance firm relegated me to a satellite office then closed it. Out of sight, out of mind. I couldn't tell Becky about getting laid off because I felt like I had already disappointed her in taking the job in the first place. I was supposed to do something nobler than selling insurance. I floundered for a few months as an independent contractor until one of my former colleagues switched to management consulting and started referring clients to me based on their risk assessments. It turned out to be a lucrative partnership, and it also gave me a business idea of my own.

I was recharged and liberated, which was one of the reasons Freedom, Kansas caught my eye. Another was that Becky's heart was set on having our own house, and real estate was a lot cheaper in Freedom than Kansas City. I had plenty of money from my investments, but I was going to need it for start-up capital. Plus, Freedom was a rural opportunity zone, so if we moved there, we'd have five years without state income tax, and the state would pay off Becky's student loans. That would be all the head start I needed. So I pitched Becky on the move, telling her marvelous things about Freedom. Money talk made her uncomfortable, so it was easy to leave out the financials.

Then I paid a visit to good old Brian to pitch my business plan. I knew through Becky that Brian was desperate to work on his research; he couldn't get a grant without a publication, but a publication would jeopardize the research. The catch-22 was perfect for me because I needed his findings to be secret. I explained to him how I would use his data to locate areas with stable energy patterns, and then sell workplace violence insurance to area businesses. Insurance is all about classifying risk, which is all about data, and none of my competitors would have the kind of information I would. I planned to set up my own company and underbid the premiums for short-term coverage, allowing businesses to opt in for a few months at a time rather than locking in for a full year or more. Ostensibly, the flexibility benefited the clients, but truly, it allowed me to watch for spikes in Brian's data then raise short-term renewal rates enough that clients would opt out before a predicted event occurred. What I saved by avoiding hefty payout claims, I would invest in energy devices or newer technology and other overhead for Brian's research, including rent for his "laboratory", such as it was.

It had all worked out perfectly, better than I ever imagined. We were flush with money in only two years, and my guilt was at a minimum. I didn't disclose information to clients who were in an area of likely violence, but I wasn't required to. And I didn't create the violence. I did provide them informal but legitimate risk management advice, so they were in better business shape when I left than when I came. Moreover, enough of them contacted me for a full risk assessment after a violent event that I started to hire associates for a separate consulting firm, eventually using insurance sales strictly to fund Brian's research.

And Brian knew about everything. He buried his head like Eisenberg's ostrich, but he knew. That's the other reason I couldn't tell Becky. She read Brian's predictions and accepted why he didn't try to help, but she wouldn't want to know how I had ruined his purity by forcing him to monetize his brilliance.

Was I bitter? Just a little.

Aiyana hadn't come back yet, so when Brian left his office, I followed him. I figured he knew exactly where Becky went, and I was right. She was sitting on the metal grating of the stairs outside the building. He sat beside her. They had such an easy camaraderie that I felt the old jealousy stir.

A patchy gray alley cat wandered beneath the stoop and reached out for Becky to pet his head. I smiled. So did Brian. "That's our Becky, beloved by creatures great and small."

From where I stood, I couldn't see Becky's blush, but it must have been there. "Beloved?" she said. "Isn't that something you say about a dead pet?" Brian laughed. He was always surprised at her humor. "What was that gory experiment Dmitri used to tell us about?" she asked. "The one with the poison capsule and the dead cat in a box?"

"Schrödinger's cat. It wasn't a real experiment; it was a thought experiment," Brian said. "And he was both dead and alive. The cat, I mean, not Schrödinger."

"So there wasn't any poison?"

"There could have been. The idea was that you wouldn't know until you looked. Except it wasn't as simple as not knowing. The cat would actually be both alive and dead until you looked."

"I didn't get it when Dmitri said it, and I still don't get it." Becky offered her self-deprecating laugh. It was a bad habit of hers, dismissing her own intelligence. The alley cat rubbed against the metal step and stretched his head toward her hand again.

"That was Schrödinger's point; it doesn't make sense. He was poking a hole in Heisenberg's uncertainty principle, which says light exists as both a particle and a wave until you measure it; *then* it becomes one or the other, but not before. The uncertainty principle, this duality, is the basis of quantum physics. Einstein didn't believe it either, although there were some things he couldn't explain."

"Thing like what?"

"Well, like action at a distance. In quantum entanglement, two subatomic particles can interact in such a way that after they are separated, when you observe one, somehow the other one 'knows', and acts the opposite. They communicate at a thousand times the speed of light. Einstein called it spooky."

"Like the holy ghost," Becky said. "Or prayer."

Brian paused for a long time. Then he said, "I'm not sure about those things."

"Aiyana still believes that you can't be a real scientist and also believe in God. Do you?"

I had seen Brian's answer hanging on the wall in his apartment. "Heisenberg said, 'The first gulp from the glass of natural sciences will turn you into an atheist, but at the bottom of the glass, God is waiting for you.'"

I expected Becky to sigh blissfully at his wisdom, but her response was more reminiscent of Aiyana. "What do *you* believe?"

Brian hesitated again before he answered. "I believe that if you look for him, he exists, and if you don't look for him, he doesn't exist."

Becky shook her head. "I think God exists whether or not you choose to see."

"Then you're in Einstein's camp, I guess. He said he preferred to think the moon exists even when we're not looking at it. Not bad company." He leaned over and bumped his shoulder to hers. "Probably proves you're smarter than all of us."

"You don't believe that."

Brian said, "I know you have more than one kind of vision that the rest of us don't. Kai tells me all the time how you're stronger than any of us realize."

I imagined she would say something to boost up Brian, remind him that he was strong and smart and the real white knight. Instead, she said, "Kai told you that?" Brian nodded, smiling as though his news should make her happy. Her voice said she took it differently. "Why doesn't he say so to me?"

The poor bastard. Becky's granny apple eyes were on him, waiting for the answer. Those eyes that were so hard to turn away from, and that you would do anything not to disappoint.

"Maybe...maybe he has a hard time...finding the words." A perfectly reasonable response, and true.

But Becky wasn't having it. "Maybe he didn't search hard enough." The stray cat shook his head and ran off into the shadows. Becky stood up. "There, now I've driven away the cat, too." She brushed her pant legs with two hard strokes, as if sweeping off the dust of our marriage.

19

Optophobia: Fear of opening one's eyes

Becky, Aiyana, and Brian were eating lunch on a break from data mining when Dmitri walked toward their table. Aiyana got up. "I don't like him. And people don't like me when I'm with him."

Brian said, "I hate to break the news, but people don't like you when you're not with him, either."

Becky stifled a grin as Aiyana left in a huff. Dmitri crossed the cafeteria with his black t-shirt taunting the other students in bold red letters: *I am not a crook. But guard your fries.* Becky didn't think it was funny in light of the current situation, which had grown worse every day in the weeks since the last bomb attempt. Vicious rumors, not always whispered, piled heavily on Dmitri.

When he walked by one table, two girls dropped their heads and focused on their straws. He turned back to them. "Do not pretend you cannot notice me. I feel you stare." He pulled a pamphlet from his back pocket and slapped it down in front of them. "But do you see what matters?" He leaned closer. "We are watching you, too." As soon as he walked on, the girls hurriedly packed up.

"What did you give them?" Brian asked. Dmitri pulled another pamphlet from his pocket and tossed it at Brian. He continued to watch the two girls. When they saw his unblinking eyes, one grabbed the paper, and they hurried out of the cafeteria.

"They think they have avoided danger in me. Fools."

Becky leaned closer to Brian to read the pamphlet. It was a Homeland Security guidance document on reporting signs of potential terrorism.

"Dude, you're compromising our project."

"Our project is to catch the bomber. Students must take responsibility."

"Yes, but you're messing with the variables."

"People will see only what they want to see. We must not allow it."

Brian took a deep breath and sat back in his chair. "Dmitri, why don't you take the night off? Becky and I will analyze the next set of data." Dmitri stood stricken, like a child on the playground whose best friend gave his toys to someone else. Becky wanted to reach over and hug the little boy, but Brian appealed to the man. "Scientist to scientist, I think you have a conflict of interest. Maybe a couple of them."

Dmitri was not immune to Brian's charms. He slowly nodded and stood up to go. Then his expression changed, displaying a tinge of desperation around the boyishness. He hesitated, as though he couldn't leave without relaying vital information. "They do not always accuse the right person." He stared at them, waiting for confirmation.

"Yeah, buddy, I know."

On their walk from the cafeteria to the data lab, Becky said to Brian, "Dmitri isn't okay."

It was a true statement, but Brian said, "He's just having a hard time with his past." He scrolled down the screen on his phone. "The data from the last twenty minutes is screwy. I think Dmitri's energy is throwing off the readings. We might have to keep him quarantined." He chuckled, but it sounded strained.

Maybe it wasn't Dmitri's energy, Becky thought. "Do you ever wonder what people mean when they say someone has 'withdrawn'?"

Brian dropped back to let some students pass. "I guess it means the person doesn't participate anymore." He fell into step next to her.

"What if it's about energy? Like the person has physically pulled back from the world?"

Brian's gait slowed, and he answered, "That's interesting, but I'm not sure energy is conscious like that."

"Maybe not." She tried a more direct approach. "Do you know about aura?"

"What, like chakra and chi and stuff? No, it's a little out there for me."

"So you don't believe people can have a visible energy field?"

"Well, if they do, I can't see it." Brian smiled indulgently and resumed his pace.

Becky could see it, but she didn't say so aloud. He was beginning to talk to her almost like an equal, so she couldn't take the risk of voicing something most people considered "out there". Even though she knew what she could see. Even though she knew that fear causes withdrawal and a person's energy coils up like a spring inside. Even though she knew that a trace of fear, like smoke, is the thing a fire leaves behind. So, as they walked, they returned to their familiar pattern: Becky asked questions about things that Brian understood, and Brian explained.

Becky wondered whether spending time with Brian should feel wrong since she and Dmitri had been getting closer. Dmitri walked her home from almost every meeting and showed up when she was alone in the cafeteria. He didn't sit any closer than he used to, but he was around her more. She wasn't sure how she felt about him, but no one so smart had ever valued her presence before. They mostly sat together in silence, and recently, the tiniest bit of his aura had started to emerge from the cold blankness. It was like coaxing a rabbit from a hole.

Although she felt intellectually inferior to Dmitri, Becky knew a lot more than he did about people. He was sweet, in his own weird way. He called her *krasivi*, Russian for "beautiful". With Brian, it was different. He was better than her in every way, and Becky felt privileged just to be around him. She knew he would never love her back; they were no more than teacher and student. Her mother had told her that one person always loves the other partner more, and Becky was willing to build a relationship on that, but Brian deserved better. She heard herself ask, "Brian, why don't you go out with Aiyana?"

Brian had been explaining something. He seemed surprised when she spoke, either by the question or by the uncharacteristic interruption. "Funny, she asked me the same thing about you."

It was Becky's turn to be surprised. "I thought she didn't like me."

"I thought you didn't like her. I guess that makes me the booby prize." He laughed.

"Oh, I didn't mean…"

He put his arm around her shoulder and gave her a brotherly squeeze. "Relax, Avery." She loved it when he called her by her last name. "I was kidding." She wished she could be that confident in herself, to be able to admit that she knew she was a prize, and not have it sound arrogant at all.

"So, why don't you?" she asked. She was restating her own question but partly wishing he would answer Aiyana's question, too.

"Aiyana and I are pals. Like you and me, right?"

She nodded and swallowed hard. Some questions are happier left unanswered.

20

March 2: 58%

I followed Brian back to the office after his talk with Becky and watched from the dark hallway while he stored away the remaining binders. His frantic pace had slowed, but he moved like a tortured animal. When he had put everything back in its place, he sat in his desk chair for a while then got up and walked toward the door. Before he reached it, he returned to the chair and dropped his head. A moment later, he got up, went to the door again. Again returned to the chair.

It was painful to see. The guy had an opportunity to be the hero that Becky always thought he was, and hell, he couldn't even make it out of the room.

A finger poked my shoulder. I knew it was Becky. She used to sneak up on campus and poke me when we first got together. Did her touch now mean she forgave me? Or was it an irony meant to hurt?

All Becky knew was that I had left like a coward in the middle of the night. She could have been holding both forgiveness and judgment in her heart. I wouldn't have to know until I turned around.

The night I left, there had been too much to explain, and my thoughts were muddled, so I had scribbled the note, hoping she would understand that it was temporary, that I was trying to fix what I could in the world where we would raise our daughter. But how could she have understood? I had hidden everything leading to that point. How could she know me when I hardly knew myself, one identity on the outside and another on the inside?

Becky was the first person I had ever tried to show both sides; I had seen the way she looked at Brian, and I envied it. So I pursued her, and our relationship did start with the same unconditional admiration. But then we became real to each other, and I imagined all of the things about me that could disappoint her. The new exposure was daunting. That's when I began to share only what I thought would make her proud. Becky might have loved me enough to accept it all, but I let my own perceptions determine our fate.

With her presence behind me and Brian's turmoil in front, my head cleared; it was time to explain. I wanted her to know everything about me, whatever the outcome. I would no longer be just an observer in our story.

21

March 2: 59%

Becky and Kai were facing each other silently in the hallway outside Brian's office. Aiyana saw them and quickly retreated, not wanting to be part of that scene. Her friendship with Becky was a curiosity, but Becky's marriage to Kai was a downright enigma. How people fit together wasn't a puzzle Aiyana was interested in solving.

She escaped to dinner at a nearby café then drove around campus and gave in to a little nostalgia. She parked near the biology building and walked to the entrance, but the doors were closed for spring break. The dark windows and empty walkways felt wrong. Unlike Brian, she didn't like being on the outside looking in.

She did understand his reluctance to get involved, considering... But he was still wrong. Putting so much work into discovering an impending but undefined danger was an exercise in futility. Or insanity. Brian was so scared of repeating an awful mistake that he was avoiding the critical piece of information: the perpetrator.

Aiyana knew the data points somehow had to be traceable back to the individual phones where they were collected. She could tweak his models using the individual data and put the bull's-eye on the person at the center of the bad energy. She would be vexed, to say the least, if such revealing information about her own energy had been obtained without her knowledge and used by someone else for the same purpose. But Aiyana could be trusted. Besides, she wasn't trying to make money; she was trying to help people.

It was around midnight when she returned to the motel. Becky was already back, and there was no sign of Kai. Aiyana tried to be quiet and get into bed without turning on the lamp, but she stubbed her toe on the bed corner.

Becky's voice came out of the darkness. "You okay?"

Aiyana grunted.

"I never stub my toe without thinking about my Sunday School teacher," Becky said. Aiyana wasn't interested in hearing why as she rubbed her foot to ease the pain. Becky told her anyway. "She used to describe Jesus like a flash of lightning in the dark, showing you where the truth is, so you don't stub your heart."

Becky had obviously been thinking about her purpose again, and forgiveness, or one of the dozen other topics that triggered her forays into religion. Aiyana normally would have made a smart remark as she rolled into bed, but in deference to Becky's hard day, she simply said, "Oh, yeah?"

"I'm not sure I believe in Jesus any more," Becky said.

"Oh, yeah?" Aiyana said again, to hide her shock.

"Well, not the same way. I've always thought of him as human on the outside only, which isn't right. Because he understood us on the inside, where the troubles start. So now I think he was sent here as a pioneer, to be the first one to recognize that we all have God in our hearts. Being Christ-like seems a little more attainable that way."

Aiyana bit her tongue.

After a minute, Becky said, "I think it's amazing how your data shows that prayer works to heal people."

Part of Aiyana wanted to keep her thoughts to herself and continue letting Becky feel better for tonight, but the bigger part couldn't turn her back on honesty. She clicked on the light. "It doesn't work the way you want to think it does."

Becky did not appear small and contemplative and broken, as Aiyana had imagined in the dark. Instead, she seemed to have grown edges since that morning. Aiyana wished, as she often did, that she could see what Becky saw, or thought she saw, about other people and their energy.

"What do you think I want to think?" Becky asked.

Aiyana took her cue from the challenging tone. Maybe Becky wasn't expecting a bedtime story after all. "Well, you want to think that because patients who are the object of prayer are more likely to respond to my energy therapy, it somehow means there is a big third party in the sky granting wishes. When in reality, any action at a distance is physics, not God. Anyway, a more likely answer is the placebo effect; they believed it would work, so it did."

"I don't think God is a genie. You know that."

"Fine, but you do insist on anthropomorphizing energy and giving it intention."

"Yes, I think there is an energy running through all living

things and connecting us. That life force is God. It makes sense to me that your energy therapy works because when people pray, they're expanding the reach of their energy fields. Like you said, it's physics."

Aiyana was too tired for such discussion. She got out of bed and crossed to the sink to brush her teeth. Her routines were way off kilter.

Becky sat up and pulled the paisley coverlet to her chin. "Do you ever think about infinity? That time never ends. Never. Ever. It stretches into big, black darkness, on and on and on, with no boundaries. Doesn't the concept strain your brain? I mean, aren't the limits of your understanding stressed at all considering the possibility?"

"No, because I believe there is an end. Death. That's it. We are not conscious of anything else, so why should infinity bother me?"

"You might not believe in an afterlife for yourself, but think outside yourself for a minute, about Life, Earth, the Milky Way, other galaxies. They will go on beyond you. They will continue to shift and die and be reborn after our sun explodes. There will be another galaxy, another cycle of life, another time, forever and ever, without end. You can't tell me that doesn't blow even your enormous capacity of a mind."

"It doesn't prove there is a God. Infinity just is."

"Exactly. God Is. You can ignore infinity, but it's still infinite."

Aiyana finished rinsing then spit her mouthwash into the sink and wiped her face. "Becky, I am never going to believe in God. I'm not. I'm never going to buy into your mythical history of death and resurrection, burning bushes, disembodied voices, genocidal floods, parting seas, and prayer."

"Okay, so you don't believe. But why do you insist that I not believe either?"

"Because it's delusional. A fantasy. If I were to see you picking bugs out of your hair, talking to yourself, and living a pretend life, shouldn't I have you committed?"

Have you committed. Guilty silence filled the room. A fly attracted to the light flittered inside the lampshade then buzzed to its death.

Aiyana sat down on the edge of her bed, facing Becky. "I'm just saying I hate to see you trying to live according to some code, straining to listen for some message, trying to divine some reason and coming up short and frustrated because it's all random in the end. When you pray, your question goes into a void. You're torturing yourself to find purpose where there is none. You might not believe this, but I don't want for you to hurt that way."

"Well, Aiyana, I see you wandering through life thinking there is nothing more to it than humans, but you're endlessly disappointed in them. You think life has no purpose, and it's a struggle keep going some days, although you won't admit it. You wonder what's the point in trying to save people, and you're angry because everyone dies in the end. You agonize over the lack of reason. I hate for you to hurt that way."

Becky reached over and switched off the light.

22

Kymophobia: Fear of wave-like motion

It was bound to happen, Aiyana and Becky on a data analysis shift together. They had both been avoiding it on the schedule—at least Aiyana had—but inevitability won out and placed them in the meeting room upstairs of the student center, facing two hours of grunt work that would be intensely awkward without talking to each other. Aiyana vowed to try to be friendly. Even if Becky attempted to convert her tonight, she would make the best of it.

The first ten minutes passed benignly. They shared some chitchat about the data and confirmed the setup then waited for the program to crunch the numbers and spit out their graphs. Aiyana fought an urge to check her email. Becky looked everywhere but at Aiyana, until she blurted, "Don't you ever go out?"

Aiyana chuckled at the bluntness. Good for Becky. "I do have friends other than you guys," she answered. It wasn't entirely true, but Becky didn't need to know that.

"Oh, well, I'm sure you do," Becky stammered. "I mean, do you date and stuff?"

So, it was going to be girl talk. Probably safer than religion. "It's too much bother to find someone who can carry on a decent conversation. There are a lot of nitwits at this school." Becky dropped her head as though Aiyana had insulted her directly. Dammit, she hadn't meant to. "What I mean is, it makes me tired to meet new people. I'd rather sit around and talk to interesting people I already know." Lest Becky take her statement as a compliment, Aiyana added, "Like Brian."

Becky's expression transformed to nothing short of dreamy. "I'd rather talk to Brian than anyone else, too."

That was a train wreck in the making. Aiyana tried to shunt the disaster. "Sure, he is a good guy, but I don't think he's interested in a relationship and all. What about Dmitri? I thought you two were kind of an item now." The graph was forming on the screen, but Aiyana let her human curiosity win out and waited for Becky's answer.

"You're right; Dmitri is sweet."

As much as Aiyana liked when people admitted she was right, "sweet" was not on her list of adjectives for Dmitri. What could Becky see in him? "He doesn't freak you out at all?" Aiyana couldn't help asking.

"He's a little intimidating, but only because he's so smart and unusual," Becky said.

"He is unusual, I will give you that." Aiyana turned her head toward the computer screen, but Becky leaned forward, blocking her view.

"Can I tell you something?" Becky said in a hushed tone.

Aiyana shrugged.

"I did his laundry."

Aiyana threw her head back and laughed. "Well, hallelujah!"

Becky cringed then went on, almost whispering. "I ironed his t-shirts and everything. Do you want to know what he said?"

"I'll bet a million dollars it wasn't 'thank you'."

"He told me that everything interesting collects in the creases. That's it, that's all." Becky held her arms out, palms up.

"I don't want to imagine what *interesting* things are in his creases," Aiyana said.

Becky wrinkled her nose and shivered off the thought.

"Maybe you can wash his hair next time. Comb it while you're at it."

Becky shook her head. "He doesn't comb his hair because it would align his brain cells, and misalignment is more creative."

Misaligned. That was an adjective for the list. "The kid is a walking freak show. He and his word for every phobia known to man. Is that some kind of party trick?"

"I can't believe you just said that!" Becky pulled off her sweatshirt to reveal a t-shirt bearing a caricature of a scientist in a bar surrounded by women staring at two slits on a board. "He gave me this," Becky said. "I don't get it."

Aiyana read the caption: *Look, it's particle. Don't look, it's a wave. Wait, look, it's a particle.* The cartoon was entitled, "Heisenberg on Ladies Night".

Yeah, the kid was definitely misaligned.

"I think he might be smarter than you," Becky said.

Aiyana looked up sharply. There was a touch of imp on Becky's face. "I doubt it," she said, smiling in spite of herself.

Twenty minutes later, they saw the pattern.

23

Hypegiaphobia: Fear of responsibility

"Why are the police calling me about your project?" the professor asked Aiyana, Brian, Becky, and Kai as they sat on the edge of their chairs in his office. The windows behind his desk contained a view of West Campus and the student center. Dmitri had not shown up for the impromptu meeting, although he was the subject.

Yesterday, Aiyana had informed the rest of the team about what she and Becky had seen: the energy change had risen beyond random and had been increasing each hour, as though people were picking up on the presence of a predator and their subconscious attention was showing up as a trail in the data. It was the pattern they had been waiting for. Brian called the police, per the agreement. The location of the pattern suggested the cafeteria was the next bomber site.

The police had indeed been receiving complaints about odd behaviors in the cafeteria—Dmitri's odd behavior. He had been handing out terror pamphlets and telling students they were being watched, and his recent t-shirts carried a string of Russian: *Astarozhnost, Apasnost,* and *Do zvisdaniya.* Caution, Danger, and Good-bye. The police said if they weren't careful, all five of them would be arrested on domestic terror charges. The other four tried to find Dmitri, but with no luck, they spent an uneasy night in their respective dorms. That morning, the police had told the professor that the teammates were under suspicion for fabricating data to complete their all-important graduation requirements.

"What the hell is going on?" the professor said again.

They stumbled over each other to explain. It had started out innocently. They were trying to do the right thing by going to the police. Brian pulled out his computer to show the professor the patterns. The professor waved him off. "I believe you have data, but it's not enough to start with a few numbers and some good intentions. That's a dangerous snowball. This project was a test of your ability to make good judgments and manage problems before we send you into the real world, and none of you have proven such abilities. So, the project ends today. Write it up, tell me what you learned, what you should have done differently, and then I will *consider* letting you graduate."

Aiyana's panic wound itself to a tight core in the pit of her stomach, and every muscle in her body contracted. Suddenly, their phones beeped in unison. Wide-eyed and unsure what to do, Kai and Becky looked to Brian. He told the professor, "The model has spiked off the charts. Something's happening in the cafeteria." The professor told them all to go home and wait while he called the police.

As soon as they left the office, Brian said, "I'm going to the cafeteria." Aiyana hesitated only a moment before she followed the others as they raced across the quad.

Dmitri was standing on a cafeteria table. His cape was draped around him, and his hands were on his hips underneath. He wasn't saying anything. A crowd had formed. His toe was pointed to a chair, in which sat a red backpack.

Dmitri glanced toward the team when they arrived and stopped inside the door. "Two hours!" he called to them. Brian stepped forward. "Two hours," Dmitri repeated in oratory to the room, "is how long this backpack has been unattended. Eighteen people"—he stamped his foot twice on the table—"saw it and avoided this area. Zero!" He stamped again. "Zero is the number who reported it."

Brian said, "Dmitri."

"We must be vigilant!"

"Dmitri!"

Dmitri threw off his cape. There was a collective gasp. In white letters on his black t-shirt were the words: *IT IS A BOMB.*

Brian stumbled backward. To Aiyana's shock and disdain, Becky stepped forward. What was she thinking? Was she trying to help Brian? To talk to Dmitri? But Dmitri wasn't paying attention to any of them. He was focused on the other students, those who were too enthralled by the spectacle to run away. "There is a terrorist at large!" he cried.

I'm getting out of here, Aiyana thought. She turned to go, and Dmitri reached for the backpack. The police surged around her. There were gunshots. Aiyana hit the floor, and Kai and Becky landed beside her.

24

Fear wants to control you. Do its bidding, act. Fear is a decision: fight or flee. My fear is in my stomach, a butterfly, a vulture. I want to flee, but I stay. I am paralyzed. Too weak to fight, too weak to run. I must do…something.

They look at me. They see through me. I'm scared to disappear. That's what they want. They don't care enough to want. I will make them respond. I will make myself fight. I will not run any more. I will show fear I am in control. I am in control.

What is suspense but fear? We live for the release. The anxiety, the relief, the escape. Escape is exhilaration.

I fear retribution. I will face it. They will not laugh.

Pay attention! See. Me. I own you now. You will remember me. Fear has no hold. I choose my own consequences. I am alone.

Fear is a wall, a door, a window. Fear is a boulder, a rock in a river. It catches sand. It grows. Life is fear. Life is feeling. Fear is Life.

25

March 3: 59%

Aiyana didn't ask Becky about her reunion with Kai as they drove back to Brian's lab and another uncertain day. She figured Becky would tell her if she wanted her to know. A construction detour took them several miles out of their way, and Aiyana's foot worked of its own accord, easing off the pedal as they passed a sign at the foot of a tree-lined lane.

"Do you ever visit him?" Aiyana asked Becky, almost against her will.

Becky didn't answer right away. The top of a white concrete building loomed above the trees. "Only once. It was awful." The dark gray roof blended with the overcast sky. "He doesn't speak."

Aiyana fought the urge to comment that it might not be a bad thing. She didn't mean it.

"It was as if he never knew me. Maybe he doesn't like to remember. Maybe not talking is his way of control." She paused. "Brian goes every week, you know."

Aiyana didn't know.

"It's why he's so…broken," Becky said. "Brian, I mean. His fear and guilt are fresh each time." The road curved, and the specter of the facility disappeared behind them. "He blames himself for not seeing it. But I also couldn't…see."

"He still thinks Dmitri is innocent, doesn't he?" Aiyana said.

"Dmitri didn't do anything wrong. We just can't prove it."

Aiyana's heart pounded with such force that she thought Becky might hear. She rolled down her window, but the warm, sticky air did nothing to clear her conscience.

Kai was already at Brian's lab when they arrived. The tall wooden table was spread with the week's updated charts, which showed a precipitous change in energy levels predicting an explosion of violence. The epicenter was definitely located in downtown Freedom, encompassing Aiyana's clinic, Becky's church, Kai's office building, and Freedom High School. While Brian explained the data, Aiyana stood across the table with Kai and Becky on either end, as if they were holding down the four corners of the earth.

"We have to tell the town it's in danger," Becky said.

"No." Aiyana and Brian were adamant.

"Telling people there is an unspecified threat, that violence could come from anyone, that the police can't help—such uncertainty would create blind panic and chaos. It will generate suspicion in all directions," Aiyana said. Her old peeves flared. "That's not going to increase the nice factor."

"People will do anything to protect what they care about, no matter how many holes are in their logic." Kai's statement rolled like dice toward Becky.

Becky's hands clutched the edge of the table. "I don't..." She took a deep breath. "I'm not sure we're the only four people in the world who can be trusted with this information."

"I don't think so at all," Brian said, "but drawing attention to it can make the situation worse. We know that." A heavy silence followed.

Aiyana was frustrated by their refusal to deal with reality. "Like it or not, we're the ones who have the information, so we have to do what we can. I think we need to mine the individual data and adjust the model to find the perpetrator."

"Aiyana, no." Brian's voice was hoarse, and he was even more haggard than the day before. "The model finds instability in energy *relationships,* in the *atmosphere,* not individuals. In the predicted conditions, with the right trigger, *anyone* can be violent."

"Then we're searching for a needle in a stack of needles." Aiyana pushed back from the table.

Yesterday, the past nine years had been, if not forgotten or forgiven, at least buried. Today, they were just beneath the surface and crying out for air.

"Aiyana, you're thinking about a town full of criminals, but it's more like a house full of gas," Kai said. "It doesn't matter where you light the match or who lights it; the whole thing is still going to explode. So our choice is either to collect the matches or to clear the air. In any case, it's not like enforcing the law after it's broken, it's more like risk management. Or preventive medicine."

Aiyana stared slack-jawed at Kai. It was the most cogent argument she had ever heard him make.

Becky's expression said she was also seeing him differently, for better or for worse. "Maybe we could do something to release stress, at least for a little while, and remind people what it feels like to be happy."

Aiyana rolled her eyes. "Bring the circus to town and the whole world will be cured?"

"Coulrophobia is a trigger," Brian said quietly. "Fear of clowns." The word hung like a cloud over the table, emphasizing the broken mirror image of the past, that their group was one member short of the first time they had tried to solve a real world problem.

Aiyana held her head high, refusing to feel the guilt. Becky seemed to follow her cue. "Then what about a concert?"

Aiyana nodded. "Music *is* useful in healing. At the right tempo, it has the properties to resonate with the heartbeat and accelerate it. Or to calm it down. The crowd atmosphere could augment that."

"Music can generate all kinds of emotion," Brian said. "Not only positive."

"Well, running it through the model can't hurt." Aiyana was tired of his defeatism.

Brian shrugged. They made assumptions about the number of people who could be reached, the percentage of positive and negative reactions, and several other key variables, and then they gathered around two large monitors while Brian entered their assumptions into his outcome model. The prediction graphs re-formed, exactly the same as before.

They generated other suggestions, but the short-term fixes caused bigger long-term problems: a free lottery whose main outcome was disappointment, a talent contest that left too many to dream, a motivational speaker or church revival or comedian, all with potential to offend. For a few minutes, they latched onto the idea of a team of psychologists providing group therapy on a large scale; but in assuming probabilities for the model, Becky pointed out how it would raise negative activity in the short term. "When you're broken, you have to go through some bad stuff to get to healing." She didn't look at Kai, but to Aiyana, her statements sounded like an acknowledgement that the couple was broken but could heal.

Becky excused herself to get a drink of water. The rest of them took the opportunity to stretch and get some distance from each other. When Becky came back, she said, "I think we need to stop looking for a one-size-fits-all solution. My kids don't come into my classroom at the same starting point, so I have to provide differentiated learning and meet them where they are. So maybe we need to do a bunch of different things at once and let people choose. They'll know better than we do what they need."

Kai nodded. "Mass customization."

They continued to brainstorm, considering everything from vacations and babysitting to debt relief, scholarships, new jobs, and buying houses long on the market—anything they could imagine that might relieve common tension. For each idea they considered, a hundred more were left unexplored. Ideas that covered the vast majority of people raised the trigger of anger for the small group left on their own. So every combination they ran through Brian's model, even with the rosiest assumptions, resulted in predictions that were the same or worse, never better. The status quo was balanced on the edge of probability, and the best they could do was nothing.

Aiyana crumpled a page of figures. "All of this hinges on the presumption that people want to be happy. But we can't be sure they'll choose the best option, even if we could give them the right choice. Some of my patients get in a state of mind where they focus on the worst in their lives and seek out things that will reinforce their misery."

Becky leaned heavily against the wall. "How would we get the money for all of this, anyway?"

Kai said, "That's my job." Aiyana glanced at him in surprise. On their project team in college, he had never offered to take responsibility. He explained his plan. "In every one of the recent patterns, petty crime has increased leading up to the mass violence, like foreshocks before a big earthquake. Theft and vandalism cost money, and the more crime in an area, the less people shop there. So, I'll go to the Chamber of Commerce with a risk management deal where they pay me to ensure a reduction in the crime rate, which I'll guarantee to give back if I fail."

"Why would anyone pay you up front for that?" Aiyana challenged. "It's pretty risky, considering we can't come up with a feasible plan."

Kai didn't hesitate when he answered, "I have a compelling track record." He breathed deeply and crossed his arms. "In all of the models, petty crime drops off after the big event; so either way, in three months, the rate will be lower than it was. If we succeed in preventing the event, we will have earned the money. If the event happens, I won't care that we didn't earn it." His gaze turned to Becky standing next to him. Any lingering doubt was erased; Kai had certainly been profiting from Brian's predictions. Becky turned away.

Aiyana's scorn churned throughout her body. It was fine for an honest businessman to make money, but Kai's methods were unscrupulous: elite information akin to insider trading, energy readings collected through a secret keyhole in a phone, and a consultancy that operated barely on the right side of the law. She would never mislead her patients just to make money. If Kai and Brian were going to act on the predictions, they should have acted to save lives.

The air in the room was heavy. Kai said, "Before you judge, consider this. Brian wouldn't even have these predictions if I hadn't funded the research." He held his arms out, inviting the verdict.

Across the table, Aiyana was quiet. The ethics of their prospects did not reach her high standards, but the alternative seemed worse. Brian slumped in a chair, his hands folded in his lap, his face blank, long ago resigned to his complicity.

Becky stood frozen in place, her eyes on the table. If she blamed Kai, she would have to blame Brian, too. "I need a shower," she said. But she stayed.

Brian looked up, startled, staring at Becky.

"Okay, so now what?" Aiyana asked, anxious to move past any guilt.

"Rain," Brian said. "Ions." He stood, suddenly more alive than he had been since they arrived.

"Brian, what are you suggesting?" said Aiyana.

"Cloud seeding."

26

March 3: 60%

"Cloud seeding? What does that mean?" Becky asked. She didn't understand why Aiyana was smiling.

"We spray silver iodide inside a cloud to make it rain." Brian's eyes met Aiyana's and he, too, began to smile. "We give the whole town a shower."

"We can't do that," Becky said. "It's not possible. It's not right." One of those statements had to be true.

Brian furrowed his eyebrows. "Of course it's possible. It's been going on since at least the 1940s."

"Where?"

"Well, leading up to the Beijing Olympics, there was a drought, so the Chinese government seeded the clouds to make it rain and clear the air pollution."

"Where in the United States?" Becky challenged again.

"It happens all over. The airports in Boise and Missoula use it to clear the fog. Rocky Mountain ski resorts do it to make snow. They use it for irrigation in California and hydroelectric plants from Iowa west. If it's done for the right reasons, it's no big deal."

To Becky, it was an enormous deal. Who decides which reasons are right? Trying to change weather is almost a sacrilege; the wind is a metaphor for God. Weather *IS,* and you live around it; you don't bend it to your will. Did people know such decisions were happening? "We can't manipulate minds that way." She shook her head and took a step back toward the wall.

"That's not what it is, Becky," Aiyana said. "We'd simply be creating an atmosphere to trigger the feel-good biology until people are conditioned to create those feelings on their own. It's like the energy therapy in my practice. It's no different from the circus or music or any other external triggers we've been talking about. It's no more manipulative than you trying to convert me to religion."

"The difference is that in every one of those things, people—you—have a *choice.* God granted free will. Who are we to take it away?"

"Maybe Becky's right," Brian said, sitting down again. "Maybe this is bordering on unethical." Maybe he didn't know what ethical looked like any more.

Aiyana stepped closer to his chair, as though she could force a physical alliance. "And it's ethical to let people die because of the ignorance of a few religious fanatics?"

Becky pushed away from the wall and held her head high, poised to leave the room.

Kai pleaded with his wife. "We have to do *something* to stop this prediction from coming true, to keep anyone we care about from getting hurt. You have to believe that the ends will justify the means."

Becky walked away. When she reached the door, she turned to unleash her anger, no longer unsure. "All I have to believe is that whatever happens, we will be able to handle it—on the inside. You may think I'm a fanatic and irrational, but it's you, every one of you, who made me that way. You made me feel guilty and afraid and desperate, believing I'd been oblivious for years and let people die instead of doing something. Then you made me feel hopeless because there's nothing we can do. You made me forget that every event is a result of free will, and prayer is the way to change a person's heart—not just the one I pray for, but my own. What we know, we know. What we can predict, we predict. But the only thing we can truly *control* is how we react to it. And I don't feel right about the reactions in this room. I'm going home." For the first time all morning, Becky's eyes were fully on Kai, as though challenging their tentative truce.

Kai pleaded again. "I can't. Not until we've exhausted all of the options…"

Becky left.

Aiyana allowed no time for second-guessing. She said, "Okay, let's come up with some assumptions on the cloud seeding and plug them into your model."

Brian glanced at the computer then the door. "I think I need to apologize, make sure she's okay…" He stood up and shuffled slightly.

"Let's do this already." Kai's urgent tone bordered on frantic. "Becky can take care of herself at the moment. Think of the bigger picture."

"I think she might be right," Brian said. "We can't stop this. We can only make it worse." He followed Becky down the hall.

Aiyana turned her frustration on Kai. "You're an idiot."

"I'm on your side!" he said.

"You should be on your wife's side. But you know what? I think she's better off without you."

"I am on her side, too, you self-righteous know-it-all. So get the pole out of your ass." Kai shoved all of their papers to the floor.

Aiyana stepped over the piles and sat down at Brian's workstation. She would figure out how to adjust the model herself.

Behind her, Kai towered over the chair. "You think you're so smart. Do you even want to understand why I can't agree with Becky on this issue, why it's more than her safety at stake? Or would you rather sit in ignorant judgment?"

Aiyana shrugged.

"Brian doesn't know this because it would paralyze him more, and Becky wouldn't want to know. Keep that in mind when, in your infinite wisdom, you think about telling either of them."

"Oh, say it already."

Kai's remaining secret spilled into the mess. "I know who the mother of our baby is."

Aiyana knew Becky would not want to hear such information. She and Kai had originally applied for an open adoption with specific parameters, but after years on the list without a match, they had finally lifted the conditions and agreed to any arrangement. So the adoption process they were going through currently was supposed to be closed to them, and breaching the privacy of the mother who was their saving grace was a line Becky would never condone crossing. It would be worse than anything they had talked about that day.

Aiyana turned around. "Who?" she asked, curious despite herself.

"I couldn't find out a name, but she's a teenager. At Freedom High School."

At the epicenter of the looming violence.

27

Fear is an instinct. Protective, nurturing, life -saving.

Fear is a warning, a guardian angel.

Fear is a surprise.

Fear is physics. Natural selection.

Fear is emotion, as old as mankind.

Fear is a motive. A locomotive. A train with no brakes.

Fear is an obstacle.

Fear is possession. Adrenaline, addiction.

Fear is a surge. A surge of relief.

The only thing to fear is fear itself.

Fear is a bullet.

28

March 3: 61%

Brian found Becky in the cafeteria, the place where they all first questioned what they knew, what they could control. She leaned on the red double doors. The cafeteria was empty except for the light in the kitchen where they could hear the janitor sweeping the floors.

"I'm scared," she said. "How can one moment change everything you know about a person?"

Brian put his arm around her. "I think knowing is from a bunch of moments, not just one."

"The bombs weren't Dmitri's. I was sure of it then, and I'm sure now. He wouldn't have put me, and all of us, in danger ."

Brian pulled her closer, and she put her head on his shoulder. He said, "He cared about you, in his own way. I guess that's the only way any of us can do it."

Brian rested his cheek on the top of Becky's head. She didn't want to move. The moment was surreal in the turmoil of the last two days, and the present and past mixed up inside her. In many ways, she still felt young and confused, but she was also ready to become a mother. "What he did wasn't personal. I mean, he was sick." She needed to talk through the feelings they never mentioned. "That did hurt, but what made it worse was realizing I was invisible. In the most important moment, I didn't matter to the people I cared about." The scene played again before them as it had so many times in their minds, though not out loud. "When Dmitri jumped off the table, and the police shot him, it was like an explosion. I saw true colors I hadn't seen before. Aiyana tried to save herself. You tried to save Dmitri. And Kai...Kai reached for me."

She pulled away, and Brian's eyes softened with apology and regret. He said, "I'm sorry for what's happening, and for what I didn't do back then. I wish I could fix everything."

Becky fell into her fantasy. She could reach up and kiss him as she had done in her schoolgirl dreams. He would love her in the best way he could. She would support him in his vulnerability. Then, when he was stronger, he would take care of her.

Even while she imagined it, she doubted. The only constant in their relationship had been her belief in him. His reaction was never the same. He had been thankful, apologetic, brotherly, patronizing. And tonight, what? She had felt many things around him, but she had never felt secure. She gazed into his sadness and indecision and loneliness, and her heart ached.

"I see a lot of things that other people don't see," she told him. Brian's eyes searched hers. She wondered if he noticed how much she had changed, too. "But I've been looking past the hero right in front of me."

She wanted to be more than a mere support to the men in her life. She disciplined and taught and took care of the kids at her school, and she would soon be a mother to a child on the way, so she needed a husband who would protect *her*, nurture *her*. Becky dropped her head and stepped out of Brian's embrace.

"Kai reached for me." She surveyed the darkened cafeteria. "He told me he loved me, right then on the floor. That was the moment." She could feel Brian behind her, but she didn't turn around. "Because he saw me. He always saw me." She was furious about Kai's secrecy and how it had stunted their relationship. Yet she also understood his fears. So, whatever else was going on, she needed first to work out their marriage. "The truth doesn't change, but our perceptions can."

29

March 3: 62%

Kai's revelation about the mother of Becky's child didn't change anything for Aiyana. Or did it? They were each convinced that they could make a difference or they couldn't, and Aiyana was the only one who knew for sure.

She couldn't tell them why, not after so much time. Could she? Too many secrets. Each of them trying to protect someone. Even Dmitri kept his silence to protect himself. And Aiyana? Who was saved by her secret?

Was Becky right? Were people entitled to know and to make their own choices? Even if their choices were wrong? Didn't they need a guide? In her head, she heard Becky's voice, or maybe it was her own. *Who are you to be the moral conscience of the world?*

Why did everyone confide secrets to her? Did they expect her to absorb the knowledge and do nothing? Well, she wasn't built that way.

30

Ouranophobia: Fear of heaven

Aiyana was on the cafeteria floor with the gunshots still ringing in her ears, and Kai and Becky were together beside her. Brian had been struck to the floor by a police officer, and Dmitri was draped over the table and part of a chair, bleeding. The police rushed forward — to stanch his wound or to cover his lifeless body, Aiyana didn't care. The other students at the edge of the cafeteria had also hit the floor. They were starting to stir and to talk.

Aiyana could imagine what they were saying. She searched for an inconspicuous way out. The police would probably want to question her again but not yet. She needed to be alone, to think about what had become of her perfectly planned life.

She eyed the main entrance to the cafeteria, but it was clogged with police, and she heard an ambulance screaming up to the building. Not a possibility. She considered climbing out a window, but that would be suspicious, plus she couldn't make the three-story jump. She scanned the metal island of cash registers. She might be able to crawl behind those and out the kitchen door. Yes, a perfect escape.

That's when she saw him. He was an ordinary kid, kind of like Brian but without the brains or charm. He was backing slowly away from the crowd, his eyes glued to the sight of Dmitri being handcuffed to a stretcher. He stepped into the corner and reached behind him for a dull green duffel bag. Aiyana's heart stopped. She had seen that bag yesterday at dinnertime. Its presence had hardly registered in her mind; it had been surrounded by backpacks, which was not usual. Whoever had designed the cafeteria had focused on coziness over function, so the small round tables had little leg space, and when the room was crowded, all available floor space was taken up with baggage. In the first week alone, one student was injured and two computers were damaged by people tripping. Since then, many students had taken to tossing their bags in the corner while they ate. Aiyana didn't trust people enough to mingle her belongings with theirs, so she rarely paid attention to the pile.

She realized that the duffel bag had probably been there the whole night. How could she have known? It wasn't suspicious at the time. Not until the kid made a point of taking it with him when he snuck out. He ducked through the cafeteria doors and out of sight.

She wanted to tell someone, but her threadbare trust of the police had been severed. *They're doing their jobs,* she heard her father say. *They're trying to keep everyone safe.* Aiyana had never felt safe; she felt exposed, always naked to the stares. She wanted to call her father and ask him what to do, but she already knew the answer. Fine, she would give the police one more chance to right the wrong.

She heaved herself off the floor. Kai was helping Becky to stand. Something had happened between the two of them, but it wasn't the time to find out what. Aiyana approached a police officer near the stretcher where Dmitri was being treated. He was paler than ever but still breathing. Aiyana felt cheated by her relief; she wanted to be angry. He didn't deserve to be forgiven.

"Miss, you'll need to step back."

"But I think—"

"We're going to question everyone here, so sit tight."

Sit tight. Oh, how she hated those words.

"I think I'm going to throw up," she said, turning toward the main exit that led to the bathroom, intending to run after the kid and command him to open the bag. What she would do if she saw a bomb inside, she had no clue.

"Joe, would you escort this young lady outside? She's going to be sick," said the officer.

Someone laid a hand on her back and led her toward the door. "It's going to be okay," he said.

She sighed, her chance for escape gone. "It passed," she said. "I'm fine."

She couldn't stop thinking about the duffel bag, but she couldn't tell the police and bring more scrutiny to herself. Besides, she wasn't sure what she saw. Reporting something that turned out to be useless could make her appear desperate, as though she were trying to deflect suspicion. So when asked, she told the truth leading up to the arrival of the police. What they didn't notice after that was their own failing.

Kai had held Becky's hand tightly through the whole ordeal of questioning, but once it was over, her face drained of color, and she started to shiver. He took her to the medical center while one of the officers drove Brian to the hospital to check on Dmitri, leaving Aiyana to wander around the quad, figuring out how to find the duffel bag kid and shake some sense into him.

Stragglers gathered around the student center, talking about the morning's events. Fortunately, everyone had been so focused on Dmitri that few recognized Aiyana. Still, she skirted around them, almost missing the kid. He was staring at the student center, sans duffel bag. His expression was blank. Either he had ditched the bag on his way out, which would have been crazy in a place crawling with police, or he had taken it back to his room, which meant his dorm was nearby.

Aiyana walked over and stood next to him. While she pretended to stare at the student center, she could feel him gawking with the corner of his eye. He shifted from foot to foot, first moving away then moving closer. It was time to take advantage of her power over the foolish male mind. "It's weird, isn't it? That this could happen on our campus?"

"Um, yeah."

"I'm in a project with the guy who did it. It's kind of scary to think we've been in danger this whole time and didn't know it." He stared at her. "I thought he was strange, but I never imagined this."

Silence.

Okay, new approach. "Did you know him?" she asked.

"No," he said, looking back at the student center.

Thinking of Becky and Kai, she said, "I guess it's hard to know anybody. Makes you think about how short and fragile life is." She nearly gagged on her own sappy words.

He was staring at her again. "Do you want to get some coffee?" he asked.

She couldn't believe her luck. Apparently, neither could he when she said yes. She told him that she wasn't in the mood for crowds and suggested they go back to his place. They didn't talk on the way to his dorm, indeed the one closest to the student center. When they got to his room, which smelled of sweat socks and microwave eggs, she saw the duffel bag. He moved it off the chair for her to sit down, nonchalant as could be. Maybe she was wrong about him. But when he set it down slowly next to the bed and pushed it under with a ginger toe, she was sure he did not want that bag to be in her line of sight or consciousness.

"Do you have any coke?" she asked.

He looked startled, as intended.

"I mean soda," she said, mustering her best giggle.

He blushed. Really? That worked?

"I don't have any," he said.

"Oh. Is there a vending machine in this building?"

"Um, no."

"No? I thought I saw one when we came in, downstairs behind the door."

"Yeah, it….doesn't work."

"Oh." How was she going to get him out of the room? She scooted from her chair to sit on his bed, brushing his leg purposely as she passed. "They must have new mattresses here. My bed isn't anywhere near this comfortable." She stretched out on her back and said, "Mmmm....cozy."

Whether it was her suggestive moves or the duffel bag underneath her, she thought the kid was going to have a heart attack. "I'm really thirsty," she said, abruptly sitting up. "I think I'll go back to my place."

"No," he said hastily. "Maybe, uh...maybe they fixed the vending machine."

"You're so sweet to check," she said. "I'm going to take a little nap while you're gone. It's been a rough morning." She lay back down on his bed and closed her eyes, though not completely.

He swallowed and glanced toward the duffel bag. She thought he might not go. "Mmmm," she said again, stretching her arms over her head, lifting her shirt a little to show her flat belly. He practically sprinted out of the room.

She leapt off the bed and peered around the corner then pushed the door closed. She shuddered off the smutty feeling then slid the bag out from under the bed. She unzipped it. Several pieces of loose notepaper were stuffed on top of two books. In between them was a bomb. Just like the picture in the paper.

Aiyana didn't know whether it was real or fake. Either way, the kid was not normal, and he could be dangerous. Suddenly, she was afraid. She rushed out the door and snuck down the back stairs.

By the time she reached her own room, her heartbeat had returned to normal, and she chastised herself for being silly. Obviously, the kid didn't have the guts to go through with anything. If he had truly wanted to blow up someone, he wouldn't have left duds all over campus. He was a cowardly attention-seeker, plain and simple.

She knew she should turn him in to the police, but he probably got rid of the evidence as soon as she disappeared from his room; she was too panicked to think of sliding it back under the bed. It would be her word against his, and she was already on the watch list. They might end up believing her, but she didn't want to get involved in a criminal case that would drag through graduation and into the start of her life.

She felt a twinge of guilt at Dmitri being in criminal custody and probably being charged with all of the bomb scares. She quickly got over it. The other backpack may not have been his, but he alone got up on that table with the intention of terrorizing people, so he could certainly benefit from a mental examination.

If she told the police what she knew, she would also have to explain why she had hunted down the kid on her own. At the very least, it would be messy. They had already disobeyed the professor by going to the cafeteria at all, and if she introduced the kid into the equation, she could jeopardize her graduation. With Dmitri being caught red-handed, the team had a neat bow on the story and could write up some lessons learned and be done with it.

To keep the kid's secret, though, she had to ensure that he would not try it again. She thought he was sufficiently scared by the blood covering Dmitri to back off and count his lucky stars. But she had to be certain.

She went to the library where she could use a computer that wasn't hers to look up class pictures and find his name. *Dennis Greeley.* She bought a package of old Christmas cards from the dollar store then addressed one to him, care of his dorm, with his room number on it. *I won't tell, but I'll be watching.* It was a little horror-movie-esque, but her note got the point across. She would keep the rest of the cards, in case he needed any reminders that he was being observed.

31

Atychiphobia: Fear of failure

The team turned over all of their data to the campus police. Since they had been in the professor's office when Dmitri had first arrived in the cafeteria, Aiyana, Brian, Becky, and Kai were immediately cleared of suspicion. The humiliation would take longer.

They still needed to write up their final report, so a week later, they met in a neutral conference room on the third floor of the faculty building. Dmitri was still in the hospital. Brian obviously hadn't shaved since they'd last met.

After forty-five minutes, they were no closer to an outline because Brian kept insisting that they should have seen it coming, before anyone got hurt. Finally, Aiyana stood up from the conference table. "Dmitri was obviously nuts, Brian. Don't beat yourself up over it." She wanted to get the project done and get the hell out of this school.

"Wake up. We caused this!" Brian said.

Aiyana turned toward the window, refusing the blame. Becky had her head down, and Kai's arm was around her. Guilt was dripping from the walls in the meeting room. Aiyana shook it off. "Did you stuff the backpack with explosives? Did you buy the materials? Did you boost him onto the cafeteria table in clear view of the police? Did you pull the trigger?"

"I might as well have," Brian said, laying his head on the table.

"I don't understand why they shot him," Becky said. "The bombs weren't functional."

"They didn't know that," Kai said.

"Well, they weren't his," Becky persisted. No one responded. "I think he was frustrated with people for not listening, not even to save themselves. I think he identified with his father who was only trying to spread the truth, too, and it made him do something in poor judgment. But I don't believe he's a criminal."

"The guy is crazy," Aiyana said, a little too forcefully. "So criminal or not, he deserves to be in a psychiatric ward. You can't argue with that." She wanted the conversation to be over.

"It was right there in the data," Brian said. "Becky tried to tell me, but I couldn't hear; I wouldn't listen."

"I should have spoken up more," Becky said. Kai's grip tightened around her.

"What the hell are you talking about?" Aiyana turned her frustration on Brian.

IIe said, "It was all about the bunnies."

Aiyana didn't understand. The bunnies?

"We were assuming the bobcat was there the whole time out of sight," Brian said, "and that the patterns showed the biomagnetic field of one predator as it escalated into an attack. But what if we take the video at face value and don't assume?" He turned his laptop around and switched on the video: the first rabbit sniffing the camera, the next rabbits stopping farther and farther away, and the bobcat turning tail to run. "If the bobcat were another bunny, what would you imagine had happened?"

Aiyana refused to answer.

"The surveillance camera," Brian answered for her. "The first rabbit saw the camera. It examined it and ran away, afraid of a foreign object. The means of observation changed the action of the observed."

"How do you explain the next two? They didn't get anywhere close to the camera."

"It's what Becky was trying to tell us, that fear causes a drawback in energy. The rabbits could sense the same thing our meter did. It was a *change*, a decrease in energy, not an increase. I don't know whether they smelled it or felt a cold spot or could see some kind of diminished aura like Becky does, but they knew. So they drew back, too, building on the trace of fear."

"You think you see *aura*?" Aiyana scoffed in Becky's direction.

"She can," Kai and Brian said together. Becky was staring hard at the computer screen, at the frozen image of the bobcat's hind leg.

Aiyana refrained from asking what color aura was around an asshole. "Fine, say the bunnies left a chill or dialed back their *aura* or whatever." Aiyana rolled her eyes. "What about the bobcat? You're going to ignore the actual perpetrator of fear in the vicinity?"

"Don't you get it?" Brian said. "The bobcat was running away from it, too. The trace of fear."

Aiyana threw up her hands. "Auras and bunnies and predators scared of a shadow? This is ridiculous. And it doesn't change the fact that Dmitri is a lunatic who is exactly where he belongs."

Brian switched off the computer and sat back hard in his chair. "You're right."

"No!" Becky said. She leaned across the table toward Brian. "He couldn't have set the first bomb because we were on the camping trip."

"It's the smoke, Becky," Brian said. "After the fire had gone. That bomb could have been set while we were still on campus. It was probably there for days before anyone called the police."

"But people must have noticed it, subconsciously anyway," Becky said.

"That's the point. We assumed the changes in our data were created by the bomber stalking the area like a predator, but what if we were actually measuring an increasing *absence* of energy, the same as with the rabbits? If people subconsciously noticed the backpack and steered clear of it, a palpable chill could have accumulated until someone consciously picked up on it. Dmitri probably understood all of this and only wanted to make people stop and think."

Aiyana pulled herself to her full height. "You're saying his nutso behavior the past few weeks was a ruse to increase awareness and get people involved? You've convinced yourselves that he's a hero?" Those kinds of thoughts would not wrap up neatly.

"No, not a hero, just someone who saw what I couldn't yet see—or understand." Brian spoke pointedly toward Becky.

She blushed and laid her head on Kai's shoulder. "It must be awful to be Dmitri and have such a great mind but not be able to communicate. It's like having a stroke, almost. You can think, but you can't make people understand."

"You're talking like the guy was a martyr. He tried to bomb the school." Aiyana waved off Becky's protests. "I don't care whether the bombs were real or not, or whether he did it once or all three times; he was crazy. Plain and simple."

"That's our fault." Brian put his head in his hands. "We created the attention, the conditions that pushed him over the edge."

"I will not take responsibility for his actions. We were trying to do the right thing."

Brian stood up and began to pace, back and forth from the table to the door. "We acted too soon. We influenced the data." The cardinal sin of science: to lose objectivity and become one of the variables. "We were so convinced that we were tracking a predator, we practically drove the police to Dmitri. He would have acted differently if they hadn't been watching him all the time. We should have waited, collected more data first."

Aiyana said, "No, it was Dmitri's frustration. Dmitri was the variable. Dmitri created the fear."

"Whatever it was, we let it happen. Then we turned over the evidence to convict him."

"Oh, well, lesson learned. Don't be too down-hearted." Aiyana's voice was over-the-top chipper, and she clapped Brian on the shoulder for good measure. "After all, the project succeeded. Our hypothesis claimed that the model would lead to the bomber, and it did. So let's write up this puppy and get on to graduation."

She tried to ignore the slack-jawed disbelief from the rest of the team. She would not let them get off track. She would proceed with her life plan, even if she had to railroad through their weak, guilty objections.

In the end, they ignored the uncomfortable what-ifs, and while Dmitri was declared incompetent to stand trial, then committed to a mental institution, the rest of the team wrote a paper about catching a predator—about catching Dmitri. Handing it in to the professor felt as foul as shoveling a mound of dirt onto a dead body.

32

Fear shouts.
Fear is fuel.
Fear is daylight.
Fear is night.
Fear is oblivion.
Fear is belief.
Fear is invisible.
Fear is dictatorship.
Fear is slavery, bondage, imprisonment.
Fear is lack of reason, irrationality.
Fear is incompetence.

33

March 3: 63%

Aiyana was searching through databases on Brian's computer, and Kai was flipping through binders and taking notes, when Becky returned to the lab. She went straight to Kai. "We're not adopting a child into the world; we're adopting her into our home. Into a place where she can feel safe from whatever is scary—in reality, or in her mind. The two of us, or the four of us, or a whole squad of us can't fix all that's bad on earth. But if you and I live with honesty and integrity, we will have the power to make a home for one little child. Please, can we do that?"

Kai stood up and enfolded her in his arms. Committed.

Out of the corner of her eye, Aiyana thought she glimpsed a bright pink glow surrounding them. For a split second, she understood: Kai gave Becky strength, and Becky made Kai visible.

"Let's go home," he whispered. Without saying goodbye, they left Aiyana alone in the lab.

Fine, Becky and Kai could go save their inexplicable marriage, but it didn't mean the town and Becky's child were no longer in danger. Aiyana would have to figure it out, to pick up the pieces of their project, again.

Meanwhile, the day's energy readings crunched through the model. The foci narrowed on Becky's school, and the probability of an event hit 65%.

34

March 3: 65%

Brian was no help at all after Kai and Becky left. When he returned to the office, rather than his usual waffling, he was more convinced than ever to do nothing.

"I thought you cared about Becky," Aiyana accused him.

He motioned her to get out from behind his workstation. "You're not doing this because you care about Becky."

She didn't move. "I care if Becky's going to get hurt."

"You care about controlling people to make sure they don't mess up your world order." He pushed her chair away from the computer.

"It protects her all the same."

"Not if the controlling can drive people to do something that puts her at even greater risk." He closed all of the files Aiyana had been studying. "You've read the data; you know taking action won't change the risk, and it might make it worse. Your drive to *do something* is about your own emotions and egotistical need to take control, not about the actual outcome. Just own up to it."

"*You're* telling *me* to own up?"

He shut down the system.

Without Brian's cooperation or knowing whether Kai's funding was still in play, Aiyana decided it was useless to stay at New Tech. She had patients and appointments waiting for her, anyway. So, she returned to Freedom with no solution and no plan.

As she rolled slowly through Main Street at dusk, she surveyed the town with its peeling paint on the courthouse, empty office spaces for lease, and shopping carts piled haphazardly in the parking lot outside the grocery store. She stopped at the light, and through the window of the diner, she saw a boy hold up a placemat to a woman across the table. The woman grabbed the paper from his hands and pushed the crayons aside, pointing harshly to his plate of food. He blinked then took a bite of sandwich and turned his wide eyes to the street outside. A waitress delivered a tray to the man and woman at the adjoining table. She set the platters in front of them, and the man gestured impatiently and heaved a whole body sigh. The waitress picked up the plates and swapped them with a soundless apology. Her thin smile disappeared as she turned back toward the kitchen.

The light turned green, and Aiyana pulled forward. She slammed on the brakes when a car passed only inches in front of her. The driver was talking on a cell phone and ran the red light. He didn't even notice how close he had come. The driver behind her beeped his horn, and Aiyana's fist curled in irritation.

When she reached her clinic, she parked behind the building and entered through the back door, hoping to hide in her office and avoid the rest of the staff until they went home.

The air inside was cold and stale, as though she had been gone a week. She flipped through her desk calendar. There were submission dates for three medical journals in the next ten days. She put her hand on the drawer that held her manuscript, printed and packaged, but she didn't open it. She wouldn't submit the article.

The manuscript described two-dozen impeccable case studies documenting her initial success with diagnostic electromagnetic scans and preventive energy therapy. It would be rejected by any reputable medical journal. The medical establishment would ridicule and dismiss her "alternative" therapies in her little rural practice. She heard her own voice making the accusations, associating her therapy with quack theories like the one she had stumbled upon recently that claimed other-dimensional beings place chemicals into human auras as a tracking mechanism, and that such interference was the cause of poor health.

Oh, please.

Aiyana's main point was not nearly so far-fetched. She simply thought it was possible to identify a physical imbalance and correct it before it produced a symptom or triggered a chain of disease. She believed pharmaceuticals had a place, when there was a true underlying defect whose natural course would be death. In those cases, a drug couldn't be worse than the disease. But she believed those cases were much more rare than mainstream medical practice would suggest.

She didn't want to buck the establishment; she considered herself part of it. She also wasn't afraid of rejection; she could counter that with data. The problem was, she wasn't facing a fair fight. Because most establishments had realized the way to get rid of something undesirable is not to object to it; it's to marginalize it. Ridicule a person out of political office. Make God the topic of a late-night comedy sketch. Frame alternative medicine in the context of witchcraft and crystals and other-dimensional beings. Confuse, deflect, denigrate—do anything but discuss the merits of a concept and give it legitimacy.

Aiyana's longest case study was a referral from Becky. The man had just turned 93 years old and was healthier than anyone that age could expect to be. He gave Aiyana a lot of the credit, but she knew the credit was mostly due to his refusal to be poisoned by fear. He had told her once, "Every body is going to die of something. That is the only certainty in this life, Dr. Rivers." He had a quiet strength, a lot like Becky.

Aiyana had learned over the years that attitude determined outcomes. So, regardless of her own convictions, she encouraged prayer for her patients of faith because when they believed it would matter, results followed.

Definitely no reputable medical journal would publish observations about prayer. She flipped the calendar pages back to the present and turned her mind to planning for the week.

The office manager had placed the next day's charts on her desk. An envelope jutted out from the pile, flaunting its return address: *B. Richter, New Tech*. If only she had picked up that envelope from the floor and thrown it away as she had intended, she would never have known the consequences of maintaining status quo. But she had lost control for one minute and was now forced to choose between doing nothing and worse than nothing. She yanked out the envelope and tore it into a dozen pieces.

35

Pharmacophobia: Fear of taking medicine

After graduation, Brian stayed at New Tech to work on an advanced degree, focusing on seismology research and earthquake predictions. Aiyana, according to plan, went on to medical school at the University of Kansas. She would have put the whole team and the final project debacle out of her mind if it hadn't been for a growing interest in diagnostic scanning and a note from Becky on the eve of her wedding to Kai.

Dear Aiyana,

I am feeling nostalgic today about the events that brought Kai and me together, and naturally my thoughts included you. I think you and I were warming up to each other near the end, and we might even have become friends in time. I would have liked that. You're different from anyone else I know.

So I thought I'd write to tell you we're in Kansas City, too. Kai is selling insurance, and I'm teaching high school. I know you're busy with classes and all, but if you ever get the chance, it would be nice to get together. Maybe I'll bake you some cookies for a study break.

Love,
Becky

Aiyana didn't know anyone else who closed letters with "Love". "Regards" sometimes. "Sincerely" most often. But "Love" was for people who cared outwardly, who put all of their messy weakness on display. People like Becky. Not like Aiyana at all.

Still, something about the message had touched her. Medical school was cutthroat; she couldn't depend on anyone. Not that Aiyana needed to depend on anyone, of course. Yet relaxing over milk and cookies with a person who didn't actively want her to fail—well, it couldn't hurt once in a while. Besides, Aiyana wasn't as sure of herself as she used to be, and Becky always made her feel superior. That was the nature of some relationships: there was always an alpha dog in the pack, but the rest of the pack was still necessary for survival. She mulled it over until one day, in a flash of weakness after struggling on an exam, Aiyana texted Becky: *How about oatmeal raisin?*

Over coffee for a brief half hour, they chatted about life in their respective schools. Turning down a second cookie, Aiyana mentioned that she didn't get as much exercise as she'd like. A couple of weeks later, Becky sent her an ad for a yoga class; she could get in for half price if she brought a friend. Aiyana cringed at the word "friend", but still she joined her. So, in ten minutes on the way to the parking lot every Tuesday and Thursday morning, the ice between them began to melt.

Then came the Tuesday that Becky ruptured her Achilles tendon during an aggressive downward dog pose. Aiyana heard the pop, but Becky didn't cry out. She sat on her mat until the end of class, when all of the other students had cleared the room, then tried to get up. Pain was evident on her face.

"I'll take you to the hospital," Aiyana said.

"No." Becky grimaced. "Take me home. It will heal."

"Don't be crazy." Aiyana helped her up off the mat. "You need a doctor."

"I don't want any medication. It's against my beliefs."

They had been successfully avoiding the charged topic. "It's against your beliefs to fix what's broken?" Aiyana pretended to be calm while she rolled up their yoga mats.

"Invasive medicine interferes with God's opportunity to perform a miracle."

Aiyana dropped the mats. She hadn't known the extent of Becky's fanaticism. "That's kind of arrogant, isn't it?" she couldn't help saying. "There are plenty of opportunities for miracles a lot bigger than little old you." Judging from Becky's expression, an observer might think Aiyana had slapped her.

Nice, Aiyana thought. Way to kick a dog while it's down. Becky started to hop toward the door, and Aiyana chided herself for her bedside manner—or lack thereof, as her advisor phrased it. She imagined the girl driving herself home, passing out from the pain, hitting her head on the kitchen counter, and leaking away her life while she lay unconscious for a week waiting for Kai to come home from his business trip.

She slung her gym bag over her shoulder and grabbed a rolling chair from behind the corner desk. Outside, she pushed it under Becky and headed toward her car. "The nuclear imaging department where I intern is always recruiting research patients. I'm sure there's a study that wouldn't require you to take drugs, so come for a scan to find out the extent of the damage. Then I'll take you home."

Becky agreed. She hardly had a choice.

At the hospital, Aiyana left Becky in the seafoam waiting room of the imaging facility and went in search of the senior resident. She explained the situation to him, and he agreed to examine Becky once he finished his rounds. If Becky needed surgery, Aiyana hoped she could convince Kai to convince Becky to do it.

Still feeling bad for being insensitive with her patient, Aiyana made an effort to be chatty while she and Becky waited. She had never been good at small talk, so she soon found herself confiding her fledgling plans for a preventive practice based on measurements of the bioelectric field. "I'm going to document bona fide case studies of people with unusual electromagnetic patterns near certain organs because I think it means they're primed for disease. If I could re-align the fields with targeted energy, I think I could prevent disease from forming."

Becky had listened but made no comment on whether she considered such therapy invasive. She did say, "Do you think the bioelectric field is what I see?"

Aiyana didn't scoff. Instead, she asked, "What does aura look like?" She had wondered about it for a long time. "I've imagined it to be like the aurora borealis."

"In a way, I guess... Think about the wavy air above the pavement on a hot day. That's kind of what I see. It's not as much on the skin as around it, and the colors aren't solid;

they're more like the color on the surface of a bubble." Becky shifted in her seat, and her face twisted with pain.

Aiyana decided to keep on talking, to keep her distracted. "Is it different for sick people? Can you see where their illness is?"

"I haven't really looked at it that way. What I see is more holistic rather than a particular area. I've read books about chakra centers related to certain organs, and they're usually illustrated with colors, but what I see isn't nearly as clear-cut as the pictures in the books. It's also not something I can look at straight on; I see it in my peripheral vision. Honestly, I can't tell the real from the fake in most of what I read, anyway."

"So it's sense more than sight?" Aiyana thought Becky might have a form of synesthesia. There had been two patients with the condition in her psych rotation. One was sure that every number and letter had an inherent color. He also thought they had personalities. The other experienced flickering lights as sounds that only she could hear.

"It's both," Becky said. "I feel a certain thing about a person at the same time as I see a certain color, but I don't know whether it started out that way or those are connections I made over time. I can definitely see intensities, though. Some auras are close to the body, and others radiate a foot or two. The clarity also changes depending on…circumstances."

They had never talked about the circumstances that brought them together. Aiyana was still skeptical of Becky's ability to see beyond the frequency of visible light, but she was on the verge of asking about Dmitri's aura, or her own, when the resident returned.

He examined Becky's calf and ankle as part of the screening protocol for the imaging study. Becky had a pen in hand to sign the consent for the MRI until he explained how magnetic resonance imaging essentially uses powerful magnets to line up hydrogen nuclei in the body and turn them ninety degrees. She refused to participate.

"They're just magnets, Becky."

"It's too invasive. I don't want my cells rearranged."

Aiyana didn't press her, so the resident said, "Well, we should at least immobilize it, to prevent further injury." Becky acquiesced. She winced when he wrapped her foot and ankle, but she refused medication. The resident gave Aiyana a prescription for an anti-inflammatory then shrugged on his way out.

Aiyana stopped to fill the prescription en route to Becky's apartment, knowing it was probably a waste of money. She returned early the next morning under the auspices of helping to feed the cats. Becky, pale but fully dressed, was clearly surprised to see her at the door. "You've got to stay off that if you want it to heal," Aiyana said, and guided her to the living room couch, where she propped up her leg with pillows.

Then Aiyana went to the kitchen to fill the cats' water bowls and pour them some food. She noticed the pet dishes were engraved. How incredibly suburbanesque. Then she read the nameplates: *Electron*, *Muon*, and *Neutrino*.

She was still laughing when she returned to the living room. "Yeah," Becky said, "Dmitri tried to explain quantum particles to me once, but all I could think was what great cat names they would make. Especially a neutrino because it doesn't like to interact with other particles and can travel right through the earth without anyone noticing. Just like a cat."

"I knew there was something I liked about those creatures." She handed Becky a glass of water and a dose of anti-inflammatory meds. Becky drank the water but refused the pills. "So," Aiyana said, "God wouldn't mind if you iced that injury a little, would he?"

Becky agreed.

The next day, Aiyana arrived under the auspices of discussing Kirlian photography, which was purported to capture aura on film. She also brought a motorized tub that she filled with ice water while Becky flipped through the photographs. "Is it the same?" Aiyana asked, easing Becky's foot into the whirlpool.

"Well, this one looks like true aura in the way x-rays look like real bone. I mean, it's there, but it's missing something. This other one is more like when a flash goes off in your face and leaves a red outline of whatever shape was in front of you. What I see isn't that at all. Anyway, at least these photos prove something is there and I'm not crazy."

Aiyana wasn't fully convinced.

The rest of the week, Aiyana didn't bother with a pretense; she and Becky simply talked. Maybe it was being in charge of a classroom, maybe it was being a wife, or maybe it was being out of college and away from the toxic infatuation with Brian— whatever the cause, Becky displayed a confidence Aiyana hadn't noticed before. It was quiet, but it was there.

Aiyana had been surprised to learn that Becky kept in touch with Brian. She showed Aiyana the heat maps he had sent as a wedding gift. He had set up his electromagnetometers around the church and showed how the energy glowed during the service. Aiyana thought it was creepy. Becky thought it was sweet, of course.

When Kai returned at the end of the week, Aiyana told him that he needed to convince Becky to get real treatment for her injury, but he said Becky's decision was hers to make. So Aiyana consulted her physical therapy colleagues and continued to visit Becky regularly with non-invasive tips and suggestions. On the day she arrived to find Becky walking normally, Aiyana couldn't help remarking, "It must be a miracle!"

Becky calmly smiled and said, "Or it might have been the doctoring."

Becky and Kai had moved to Freedom shortly thereafter, where he opened his own insurance business, and Becky started teaching at Freedom High School. Aiyana was inspired and ruminated on how soon she could have her own practice. Her experience was limited, but she desperately wanted to put her energy therapy to the test. So when Becky sent her the advertisement soliciting a doctor to take over an existing practice in Freedom—including a year of transitional mentorship plus pay-down of her school loans— the friendship became inevitable.

When Brian dropped out of his seismology program to conduct his own energy research with private funding, Aiyana was surprised to find his first letter in the mail. She opened it and read about the patterns in his initial data from Canada and his first prediction of a violent event in Saskatchewan. She was caught off guard by the guilt that resurfaced, and she was apprehensive for months afterwards, uncertain about what to do and whether to intervene. She was both angry and relieved when he turned out to be wrong. The letters continued to arrive periodically, but she told Becky to tell Brian she would never read another one.

36

March 10: 70%

Since the reunion at New Tech had ended so fruitlessly, every day felt aimless. There was no resolution to the lingering threat, the unrequited relationships, the half-healed wounds, or Dmitri. Every day was filled with indefinite waiting.

The four tried to disregard it and focus on things they could control. Becky and Kai trod carefully around their reconnection. Aiyana continued with her practice, ignoring the manuscript in her desk and Becky's inquiries about it. None of them talked to Brian.

Becky's nerves were coiled like springs. She finally understood why energy pent up inside was called potential: She had the potential to turn kinetic at any moment. She wondered where her transformation point was. Could she, like Dmitri, become the perpetrator? What about Aiyana, whose irritation had always been close to the surface?

None of them needed data to feel what was happening around them. It was the same as ever, in many ways, only more frequent and overt: swearing in traffic, sighs in checkout lines, collisions without apologies. They heard the frustration in snippets of conversation: "Someone cut in front of me, and I wanted to yank her by the hair… They talked all through the movie and no one did anything about it… I got passed to eight different people before I hung up. Worst customer service ever… My boss took my idea and used it like his own, but what could I do? I need the job…"

All over town, petty frustrations overwhelmed the joy and importance of life. There were days when even Becky wanted to smash something, feeling so helpless in the face of it all. Babies wouldn't stop crying. Parents yelled at their children and strangers' children, too. Half of the graduating class was functionally illiterate, but few seemed to care.

The whole town felt on the verge, but no one knew of what, or who might be capable of doing it.

37

March 12: 71%

While her students worked on their in-class assignment, Becky studied the girl in the front row. An anemic blue glow surrounded her, muted and dark, as it had been for weeks. It was the same for all of the students, in degrees.

Dillon had it the worst. The air about him was cold and opaque, as though he had no light inside at all. He sat in the back row, withdrawn completely upon himself. The other kids walked a bit faster in front of him. Each day, they inched their desks slightly farther away, hardly realizing what they were doing. He still walked the hall with a couple of friends, but there was a distance between them.

Becky shivered. She had only witnessed such behavior once before, with Dmitri.

She noticed a crescendo in the shuffling and shifting, as though the bell were soon to ring, but there was another twenty minutes yet of class. Becky had visions of waves withdrawing to the sea, signaling a tsunami.

38

March 15: 72%

On the Friday two weeks after their trip to New Tech,
Aiyana had a full schedule of patients and a backlog of
paperwork, so it was ten o'clock by the time she arrived home
to her brownstone. She hung her key chain on its hook and
crossed the living room with its hardwood floors and
minimalist style, devoid of expressions of her heritage or
pictures of family or anything that would box her into a reality
she hadn't chosen. She made herself a cup of tea and mulled
the day over in her mind.

Her patients' diagnostic scans had all registered their
weakest levels since she had started measuring them. But
relatively speaking, they were in balance. There were no
particular areas of skew that she could force into alignment
with a beam of ions or magnetism or heat. Their bodies were
simply primed for illness anywhere and everywhere, like the
world outside.

It was hard for Aiyana to send her patients home without a
recommendation, and she told as much to her 93-year-old, her
first case study. She often found herself telling him things she
didn't share with other patients. He was comfortable to be

around, and her receptionist left extra time in his appointments because he liked to talk. Today was the anniversary of his wife's end-of-life discussion with her doctors. They had said her cancer was terminal, and there was no more they could do. He had wanted to keep fighting: money was no object, there was always another opinion, he could be brave enough for both of them. His wife had wanted only for him to recognize that the time had come to stop fighting. "It's been ten years since she passed, Dr. Rivers, and I'll tell you what. Acceptance was my greatest act of courage."

Aiyana set her cup on a stone coaster on the missionary table next to her reading chair and knelt to the floor beside a carved wooden trunk. She opened it and pulled out a stack of Christmas cards and a painting. Bright yellow, orange, and blue geometric print surrounded an eagle with wings of fire, and Aiyana's name in Chinese characters adorned the frame. It was her parents' artistic attempt at fusing their cultures, but to Aiyana, it put them more in contrast than ever. Her maternal grandmother was half Kiikaapoi and half Pottawatomie and her maternal grandfather was from the village of Wuyuan in the Jiangxi province of China. Aiyana's father had been fascinated by the specifics of her mother's heritage. He had studied much about West Africa to understand his own roots, but he wasn't able to trace his ancestors back to a particular part of the continent. That's why he, even more than her mother, had wanted Aiyana to grow up on the reservation, where at least part of her culture would be living around her.

Aiyana resented her acute awareness that no matter where she was the rest of her life, part of her wouldn't fit in. So she hadn't hung up the painting, not wanting a reminder of the discord within herself. She had stuffed it down, increasing the friction, until her resentment and anger boiled to the surface.

Her high school on the reservation was one of the most innovative in the country, but growing up, she was focused on getting out, and away from the weight of all the culture she was expected to carry. When she had shown her parents her full merit offer to New Tech University, they were happy for her. Acceptances to Harvard, Stanford, and Caltech also came, but there wasn't a diversity scholarship among them, so Aiyana had to admit that she had declined to reveal her ethnicity on the applications.

Her father had asked her why. He truly didn't understand. She needed to know colleges wanted her because of who she had made herself on the inside, not how she was born on the outside. Her father told her that the two are inseparable; they mold each other. He said a person's inside has to grow big enough to push its way out. He was proud in the best sense, like a lion, and it glowed from him. People who mattered saw that first, and Aiyana knew it. Still, she argued. *People only see what they want to see, and they judge you by that; it isn't fair. Aiyana, don't worry about how other people act; you can only control how you react.*

She had never taken his advice to heart, and he was saddened by her struggle against perceptions she couldn't change. He and Becky were alike in that way. She hadn't realized it before, but they were alike in a lot of ways, including their religion. It was probably what irritated her in the beginning. Her parents' marriage was very different from

Becky and Kai's, but it was also an unlikely union, as was her friendship with Becky.

Aiyana pushed herself up from her knees. She put the box of cards on the table and picked up her cup of tea. Her left hand tipped the cup to her lips while her right hand set the painting on the mantle above the fireplace. Maybe the time had come to accept the unlikely union inside herself and display all of the person she was. She stepped back and took another sip. The art changed the whole feel of the room, though for worse or better, she wasn't sure. She made a mental note to call her parents in the morning.

She picked up the box again and pulled out one card and one envelope and threw the rest in the wire wastebasket. Bygones needed to be bygones. *From you know who.* She wrote it one last time and slipped the card inside the envelope.

She went upstairs to her home office and switched on the computer and opened her address book. He had moved around a lot in the past nine years, but she had always located him. She typed *Dennis Greeley* into the online finder, and she recognized last year's address on the list: Eureka, Kansas. That's where Brian was from. Aiyana remembered because he said that growing up in a town called Eureka, he almost felt destined to become a scientist. She hadn't bothered in the past to find out what Dennis Greeley did for a living, but since it would be her last contact, she was curious. A quick search pulled up a partial resume. He was a guidance counselor; she hadn't expected that. Then she saw his new address and current job—at Freedom High School.

39

Fear rumbled and undulated, traveling impatiently across the earth.
Beneath their feet, below their consciousness.
They didn't believe that it would surface, but it would.
Fear would.
Erupt.

40

March 18: 73%

"I have to say I was surprised to get your call. It was kind of out of the blue," Becky said as she and Aiyana walked to the entrance of Freedom High School.

"Well, we had talked before about showing your classes my research, and I remembered you said you would be making magnetometers at some point, so since we haven't talked in a while, I thought…"

Becky wasn't convinced by Aiyana's seemingly innocent reasons, but she had her own reasons for wanting the visit. "Okay, well, thanks for bringing the scanner today. I thought it would engage the kids more than a talk."

They pushed the scanner through the double glass doors. A uniformed police officer stood to the right inside the entrance of the school, watching the students intently as they filed in. Another officer was searching backpacks and duffel bags as their student owners passed through a metal detector.

Becky tensed visibly at the sight of it all. Aiyana thought the metal trellis, although not necessarily ominous, was out-of-place against the backdrop of brightly colored posters advertising an upcoming bake sale.

The officers gestured Aiyana and Becky around to a separate entrance where the scanner underwent a cursory inspection. Aiyana offered her purse for inspection as well, but the officer waved her through.

She watched a group of teenage girls whispering animatedly as they climbed the stone steps. She expected them to become solemn as they neared the police officers, but they handed over their bags and continued their conversation around the trellis as though it weren't even there.

"The kids take it in stride, don't they? Going through the metal detector?"

"That's the worst thing about it," Becky said. "They think it's normal to be under suspicion." Her mouth was set hard in a way that Aiyana had never seen before.

They stopped in the administration office to register Aiyana as a guest, and Becky's dark mood disappeared as she gaily greeted the office workers and introduced Aiyana as her "best friend from college". Aiyana didn't consider herself the "besties" type, and she and Becky weren't really friends in college, but she put on her doctor-to-patient smile and said hello.

She clipped on her visitor's badge as they weaved their way through the clang of locker doors and the students milling about before the starting bell. Aiyana read more of the posters on the walls: announcements for the spring musical, encouragement for pending tournaments, and crisis hotlines.

Becky's classroom was not exactly what Aiyana expected. One wall was plastered with pictures of famous scientists, tacked over with little known facts researched by the kids.

Another wall was papered with various colored bar charts and pie graphs and scatter plots, like a museum of modern art. A sideboard under a wall of windows running the length of the classroom was filled with student science projects. In the corner was a collection of soda bottles and pickle jars strung with magnets and laser pointers. Aiyana recognized them as homemade magnetometers.

Becky pointed her to the back of the room to set up her scanner on one of the eight impeccably cleaned black worktables. Each table was equipped with a sink and gas spout. "You have lab benches," Aiyana remarked with surprise.

"Well, I am a science teacher."

"I know, I just never thought about your classes actually doing experiments. I mean, you teach mostly freshmen, right?"

"Kids have to know a lot more than they used to. Complicated world and all. But don't worry, I know what I'm doing."

"I'm sure you do," Aiyana said, and realized that she believed it.

"I'll start by telling the kids our plans for the day then hand the class over to you to give a short description of how your device works in your medical practice. Then we'll do the measurements. I encourage questions, which should take most of the second half of the period. Afterward, they'll go over to their biology class and continue the lesson. We have two periods before lunch, then three more this afternoon."

Aiyana didn't say so out loud, but she was impressed by Becky's efficiency. It hadn't occurred to her before, but she supposed efficiency was necessary to be a teacher, with days broken into timed segments and a new group of students passing through every hour, bringing their assorted histories with them. It was a lot like her medical clinic, except Aiyana only treated one person at a time, and she had staff to help.

The bell rang, and kids spilled into the classroom, taking their usual seats. A muted chatter continued until Becky softly said, "Good morning." Aiyana expected the kids to keep right on talking, but they fell quiet immediately.

Becky collected permission slips for the day and conducted other housekeeping requirements then launched into activity mode. "Okay, remember last month we learned about protons and electrons and electricity, and last week we made the magnetometers to study the fields of the earth. Well, today Dr. Rivers has brought a device that she uses to measure the magnetic fields of a person's body." She pointed to the device at the back of the room then laid a hand on Aiyana's shoulder. "This is Doctor Rivers."

A smattering of voices said, "Hi, Doctor Rivers."

Aiyana waved. "Hi."

"You'll each have the opportunity to be scanned and get your own personal report, which Doctor Rivers will help us to understand. You'll also have a chance to compare your results to the average results for the class. We'll add those to our graph collection. Then next week, in here and in your biology class, we'll be studying how your body makes electricity and the ways that biomagnetic fields are alike or different from the magnetic fields of the earth. Doctor Rivers?" She gestured to Aiyana.

"Okay..." Aiyana was disconcerted by the experience of Becky in a position of authority. "Well, when patients come to visit me, we do a whole scan of their bodies to measure the strength of their biomagnetic fields, and we map them onto a picture. We do that whenever they come into the office, so we can track changes over weeks or months or years. For example, if a person's stomach area starts showing up with a weaker energy field compared to the rest of her body, it might mean her stomach is getting a disease, even if she doesn't feel sick yet. We call this a 'diagnostic' scan, and it's what we'll do today. We're only going to measure your hands, though, because I couldn't get a whole body scanner through the metal detector." She smiled, and a couple of the kids smiled back.

"All right," Becky said, "the team that won the challenge yesterday will go first. Everyone else can get in line as soon as you know the answers to the questions on the board." She pointed to a list printed on the computerized board at the front of the room:

> ➤ *What causes high and low tides in the ocean?*
> ➤ *Aside from hydrogen and oxygen (H_2O), what are the two most common elements in the ocean?*
> ➤ *What is the most common element in the earth's core?*
> ➤ *What magnetic element is found in human blood?*
> ➤ *How many protons and electrons are in a neutral atom of iron and why is it neutral?*
> ➤ *What is an atom with a charge called?*
> ➤ *What are the names of the two charged atoms that form an ionic bond to produce table salt?*

"You can help each other on this, and try to notice something interesting about the answers. We're going to talk more about these during the week. Oh, and if you're going to use the internet to look these up, remember to consult your list of ways to determine whether your internet source is reliable." She pointed to another printed list tacked on the wall next to the board.

The students moved slowly to form their pairs while several lined up shyly in the back next to the scanner. Aiyana directed them to run their hands through the machine, and she handed them their printouts. A few mumbled thanks as they returned to their seats. Aiyana was surprised to find their energy levels were lower than her patients'. She had somehow expected younger people to be more intense, although the assumption was not based on any evidence, considering she generally steered clear of children.

Becky prompted a few questions that the students dutifully asked, but they were sluggish like coffee addicts at the crack of dawn. The last boy's report came out blank. There was an outline but no shading and all zeroes for the results. Aiyana passed his hand through the scanner again, but again the report was blank. She had Becky pass through, and the machine printed a multi-colored array fit for analysis. Aiyana was stymied. The boy, Dillon, fidgeted while the other students stared at him from a distance. She wasn't sure whether he wanted to hit her or run out of the room and cry.

Becky said, "Doctor Rivers, do you think some people might keep their energy close inside, so the machine is not strong enough to pick it up?"

Aiyana said, "Yes, I bet that's what happened." The boy relaxed and took his two blank pages back to his seat.

In the next class, Becky started with a video that had gone viral the day before. Aiyana didn't pay much attention as she reset her equipment, but she heard the kids laughing uproariously even after the video ended. Becky wound them down and brought the class back to order, with a lingering giggle here and there.

The readings for the second period students were markedly higher than the first period, and the students bombarded Aiyana with questions. As they filed out at the end of the period, she heard some thought-provoking, if not entirely correct, conclusions. "If people have magnetic fields, they can actually be attracted to each other. That means love is, like, scientific."

When all the students had gone, Aiyana stood before Becky's desk in accusatory stance. "You wanted me to do these scans for a reason, didn't you?"

Becky shrugged and passed her a homemade burrito and a carton of milk. "It's the darn metal detector."

Aiyana found it quaint the way Becky still used "darn" when only the two of them could hear.

"You know the administration wanted to black out the windows and teach the kids self-defense? Here and in the junior high, too!"

Aiyana recalled the argument from months before, prior to the start of school. "So?" Aiyana egged her on. "They're trying to keep the kids safe. Before the school violence happens here. Besides, people should be able to protect themselves."

Becky shook her head vehemently. "A ten-year-old should not have to be responsible for his or her own safety. Nor a fourteen-year-old or a sixteen-year-old. It should not be an option for us to anticipate failure and use self-defense as plan A. If we can't keep kids safe, we shouldn't force them to come to school."

Aiyana didn't remember Becky being so passionate about the topic before. Had her ire been building, or was it stirred up by the predictions?

"I can get over the guards," Becky went on. "I appreciate the statement they make: We're the adults and we're here to protect you. But the metal detector says something quite different. Every kid is put through it every day, which says: there are criminals among you, and you're apt to become one yourself. I try so hard to help them find their positive potential, but any momentum is cancelled out the very next morning. As if teenagers don't have enough to handle, with intense feelings, peer pressure and cyber-bullying, trying to understand new concepts for hours on end, not to mention whatever is going on outside or at home. They don't need a big metal reminder of the darkness among them. I've seen classes get more and more withdrawn since the beginning of the year, and the kids are either lackluster or fidgety, but all I can think is that I don't blame them. Have you ever tried to learn when you're afraid of the person next to you, or in your own seat?"

Aiyana had felt safe in her little high school, so she couldn't relate to present-day teenagers, although she wondered whether her safety had been merely an illusion. She knew that a fight or flight response to fear turns off a brain's capacity to retain information. She didn't perceive an active fear in Becky's students, but anxiety was a close cousin, and she had seen how chronic anxiety could be masked on the surface, even to the patient. "What is the laughter supposed to do?"

"I read in a magazine about groups of people who get together and laugh for no reason, as a stress release. I wanted to try it."

"And you wanted me to measure it."

Becky shrugged again, with a twinkle in her eye.

Aiyana wondered if it would work. When her patients were in pain, she focused on taking away the cause; she assumed that any related fears would go away as soon as the pain did. When she thought about it more closely, though, she realized patient scans often showed a pattern of residual anxiety, a depressed magnetic field persisting after all of their physical signs were back to normal. There was something important in the revelation, but Aiyana couldn't quite put her finger on it.

The next two classes were subdued like the first one, but in the final period, Becky triggered the laughter again, and again, the energy levels increased.

While the students were lined up for the final bell, a girl with dangly earrings and a wealth of bracelets strung with colored stones asked Aiyana what she would do *after* the diagnosis if she found an area that had weaker energy compared to the rest of the body.

"If people feel sick," Aiyana explained, "or have any other symptoms, we run more tests to figure out exactly what's wrong and treat it accordingly. If they don't feel sick, or if no other treatment works, or they don't want the other treatment" — she looked pointedly at Becky — "then we use electromagnetic energy therapy. That's where we turn a beam of light or negative ions or electrons onto the particular area for about fifteen minutes a day until the readings go back to normal. The energy kind of breaks up stagnation to jump-start the healing system in your own body."

"Is that like magnetic bracelets and crystals and stuff?" the girl asked.

"No!" Aiyana said, more harshly than she intended. "No," she repeated, softer but still adamant. "It's a carefully developed therapy custom-designed for the patient and targeted only to a specific area." *Not a generic piece of junk anyone can buy off the Internet.*

Unperturbed by Aiyana's tone, the girl said, "So, you put a magnetic field on people who are sick to make them better?"

Aiyana hesitated then said, "Essentially, yes."

"And I have a magnetic field all over my body, including my hands?"

"Yes." Had she not been paying attention for the past hour?

"Then why can't I put my hands on someone who is sick and make them better?"

Aiyana stifled the urge to sigh. "The magnetic field in your hands isn't quite strong enough to do that."

"Jesus did it."

Aiyana was not prepared for this discussion. She appealed silently to Becky, who was leaning against a wall with her eyebrows raised, apparently enjoying the exchange. Aiyana said, "Jesus lived a long time ago, so I don't have any measurements of his magnetic field."

"The guy in the revival tent did it last weekend in Kansas City."

I'll bet he did. "You send him on down to my clinic, and I will be more than happy to measure his hands."

The bell rang, and the students swarmed to the exit. Aiyana breathed a sigh of relief. She turned her attention to her real reason for the visit. "Is the guidance counselor around? I have some questions about his work, while I'm here."

"Who? Dennis Greeley?" Becky's expression was wary. "Do you know him?"

"Oh, well…I know he went to New Tech."

"He's never mentioned that he knew you."

"We don't really… Why would he, anyway? He barely knows you either, right?"

"Brian's known him for years. He recommended him for this job."

Aiyana couldn't hide her shock. "What? Why?"

"He sees him on the weekends when he visits Dmitri. Dennis volunteers in the mental facility." Becky squinted her eyes. "Are you sure you didn't know?"

Aiyana didn't have to lie. "I had no idea. I've never been there."

"Oh." Becky's suspicion dissipated. "Anyway, Dennis is out for a couple of weeks. He's getting married on Saturday."

41

March 23: 74%

On Saturday morning, Aiyana sat in her car outside the church and watched the wedding guests arrive. She hadn't yet determined when she would pull the bride aside and tell her that her soon-to-be husband was a would-be bomber. She had to do it, though. It was for the woman's own good. She ought to know him before she married him.

Aiyana waited until the last car arrived, but still she didn't go in. She couldn't bring herself to interrupt the ceremony. What if nine years could change a man? Her uncertainty was growing, and it bothered her.

After the bride and groom left the church in a parade of bubbles, Aiyana finally got out of the car and followed the last group of guests across the lawn to the reception hall. She ducked into a corner to watch while the newlyweds circulated about the room. Dennis and his new wife were visibly giddy. Aiyana felt a twinge of jealousy followed quickly by a desire to vomit. She slipped out the back door to the parking lot, intending to leave well enough alone, until she heard a voice behind her.

"Aiyana Rivers." It was Dennis Greeley. He was walking down the stairs toward her. "I thought you might come. I almost sent you an invitation, actually, but I couldn't figure out how to explain it to my wife." He laughed nervously and stopped on the bottom step. "I wanted you to know...I'm not the same person any more." He rubbed his palms on his tuxedo pants. "You saved my life." He held out a hand. Aiyana considered refusing to shake it, but his contrition was what she had intended, wasn't it? "I was so angry, so invisible, until you sent those cards. I went to counseling. I'm a counselor myself now."

"Your wife doesn't know?"

"She does. I told her when we first got serious about five years ago. We agreed it's in the past; there's no need to talk about it any more."

His tone wasn't pleading or duplicitous, yet Aiyana found it hard to believe that a person could know something hideous about another person and still want to share her life with him. The couples she knew only married because they made the commitment before they opened the closet. "I'm glad for you." She didn't know what else to say. "Why the five-year engagement?"

"Oh, well, we didn't originally intend to get married, but it came time to...set an example. For our kids. Her kids." He shifted from foot to foot and a bead of sweat dotted his upper lip. "We didn't tell them. About what I did. Maybe when they're older, I can explain..."

Aiyana experienced a baffling inclination to set him at ease. She didn't know the kids, so what could a promise hurt? "Don't worry, they won't hear it from me."

"Thank you."

"You're welcome."

"No, I mean it. Thank you."

42

Fear sat on a mountain surveying his handiwork. I own you and you and you.

Just then, a boy scrambled over the highest rock and pulled himself up to stand before Fear. "You will not own me," said the boy.

Fear regarded the boy, almost with respect. "Your courage is admirable. But courage has no definition except for me. By naming me, your life is mine."

The boy planted his feet firmly on the ground. "I am the master of my destiny."

"You master nothing! You made this journey to face me. Therefore, I control you."

The boy turned to go.

"You flee from me!" cried Fear. "I am your compass."

The boy continued down the mountain as deliberately as he came. But not as sure.

He passed a farmer on his way from the mountain. "Are you not afraid that your crops will wither?" asked the boy.

The farmer said, "Fear is a famine. I feed the hungry."

He passed a fireman. "Do you not fear that you will burn to ash?"

The fireman said, "Fear is a fire. I rescue."

He met a doctor. "Do you not fear that your patients will die?"

"None conquers death," she said.

The boy met an angel, and he cried. "I fear I will lose my family to famine, that they will burn, or die. I could not battle Fear. Yet I cannot run far enough away."

The angel said, "Be not afraid."

Then the boy met a girl. She had skin of sugar and hair of spice. "Do you go to the mountain to meet your destiny? To conquer fear?" he asked.

She regarded him curiously. "I know not Fear. My name is Faith. Who are you?"

The boy felt a glow inside, and her atmosphere filled the air. "I do not know," he said. "But I am not Afraid."

43

March 25: 75%

Becky heard Kai's car pull into the driveway. She set her students' papers aside and went to the kitchen. He was reading his phone as he entered, so he didn't notice her standing in the doorway between rooms. He switched his phone from his left hand to his right as he took off his suit jacket and tie and loosened his shirt; then he set the phone on the counter. She watched him stretch from shoulder to shoulder, his neatly trimmed hairline accentuating the strong tendon that ran under his collar. He reached into the cupboard for a glass, and she felt herself smile.

While he drank his water, she snuck up behind him and slid her arms around his chest, pressing her face to his back. He chuckled in surprise and covered her hand with his. His arm was warm on hers, and she sighed.

"What's going on?" he asked, turning around and wrapping her in an embrace.

She looked up into the dark glass of his eyes, like a tunnel between their souls. Her heart swelled and sent up a tear. "I'm just glad to see you."

His eyebrows furrowed for a second then he pulled her close. "Are you okay?"

"Mm hm," she hummed into the warmth of his chest. They stood together for several minutes, their breaths moving between them in harmony.

Then Kai said, "I hate to break this up, but I told Joe I'd go over to his place and check the stove. Mary's been worrying that she didn't turn it off when they left for vacation this morning." They pulled apart, and he hesitated before saying, "Do you want to walk over with me?"

She nodded, and he smiled.

Kai changed his clothes then they crossed through their neighbor's cornfield that served as the boundary between their houses. The stalks were high despite the drought, and the floppy green leaves curtained their path. Kai walked next to Becky with his left side forward, lifting the leaves for her to duck under, like a dance.

Inside their neighbors' house, they surveyed the kitchen then Kai dialed his phone. "Hi, Joe? Yeah, the stove's off, no need to worry." He listened for a moment and nodded. "Sure we can, no problem." He turned off the phone and chuckled. "They left a load in the wash."

They searched for the laundry room in the pantry and the basement, but they couldn't find one. So they climbed the stairs to the second floor and found the washer and dryer tucked into a closet in the master bedroom. Becky shifted the damp sheets and towels from the washer to the dryer. They agreed that they shouldn't leave the dryer running unattended, so Becky took a seat on a vanity bench while Kai hopped onto the washing machine to wait.

Becky looked out the window to their house in the distance. It felt strangely good, being in someone else's home.

"It's nice getting outside of our life for a change, isn't it?" Kai said. Becky breathed deeply and nodded. "Crazy couple of weeks."

Several minutes passed with no sound but the rumble of the dryer and the occasional knock of Kai's sneaker dangling against the washing machine. Then he said casually, "No one's home. Empty room. Nice, cozy comforter."

Her head snapped toward him. He had a twinkle in his eyes and a grin tickling the corners of his mouth. "Kai!" she said, heat rising through her.

He shrugged. "Just thought I'd mention it."

The memory of their wedding night filled the room. His parents had insisted on a lavish evening soiree, well beyond what her mother and the young couple could afford. It was a source of tension early on, especially between Kai and his parents, but the couple eventually gave in. Becky was swept away by her dress with its long white velvet sleeves and cascades of silk, and a guest list filled with people who had shaped the person she was, whether they knew it or not. She had expected less than half of them to come, but the RSVP's had poured in yes after yes after yes. She hadn't dared to invite Aiyana, to provoke a scoff and certain decline, but the night before the wedding, Becky felt bold. Not wanting any regrets at the beginning of her new life, she had written a note to Aiyana then ran to the mailbox before she could change her mind.

The morning of the wedding was a blur, but the night of the event stood out in sharp perfection. Brian's presence was a mere peripheral event; her heart was focused on Kai. Becky knew that God was truly binding them together when her minister's eyes glistened after the vows. The reception had lasted until one in the morning, and Kai and Becky drove all night to Denver for a direct flight to Hawaii—a honeymoon gift from his parents in apology for the initial tension.

They sprung two flat tires on Route 70 halfway to nowhere, so they were late arriving at the airport, and their seats had been given away by the time they made it to the gate. The flight crew felt bad for the newlyweds and fudged the waiting list to get them on board, but in two separate seats. It was okay because they had intended to sleep the whole trip anyway, but a colicky baby and a rowdy group of surfers changed their plans. When they landed in Hawaii, they reunited on the exit ramp, bleary-eyed, yet still the blissful newlyweds, kissing during the entire taxi ride to the hotel in desperate anticipation. Kai had waited like a gentleman from another century to fulfill her biggest fairy tale, and Becky was eager to share the experience with him at last.

At the hotel, they were told they couldn't check in yet. The newlyweds who were occupying their suite hadn't yet checked out because they had been left behind on their final hike up a volcano. The next bus to get them wouldn't be for several hours, so, with fingers intertwined and eyelids heavy, Becky and Kai spent the afternoon drinking complimentary mai tais on a bamboo balcony overlooking the turquoise ocean.

When they were finally allowed to check into their suite, they found it to be well worth the wait, especially the huge bed with its comforter like a cloud from heaven. They both collapsed onto it, and half-drunk, they fell asleep. Becky woke up to the moon shining brightly across their bed and Kai curled around her. She watched him for a while, savoring the sweet realization that "she" had become "we" forever, then she woke him with a kiss.

The dryer buzzed, bringing Becky back to the present. Kai hopped off and emptied the machine and dumped an armful of linens on the bed. Becky got up, and they grabbed two towels and started folding.

"One of my clients renewed his contract today," Kai said.

"Really?" Becky said. "You must be doing something right."

"I guess." He reached for another towel.

"One of my students got a perfect score on the state science exam."

"Of course, you're a great teacher."

She grabbed another towel. "I wish I could take the credit."

"But....?"

"Sometimes I think it doesn't matter how good of a teacher I am; kids are going to get it or they aren't. I mean, there's one boy who sits in the back and spend most of the time inside his own head. His stepfather is the guidance counselor, so if he can't help him, I don't know what I can do. He acts like he wants to be invisible." Becky pulled out a sheet, and Kai took one end, backing up to the door to shake it out before they walked toward each other.

"Nobody wants to be invisible," he said. They stood face-to-face and palm-to-palm, holding the sheet between them.

"He isn't," she said, lacing her fingers with his.

They finished the laundry, flipped off the lights, and locked the house behind them. When they emerged from the cornfield to their mowed back lawn, Kai slipped his hand in hers, and they walked up to their house together.

"We should get going on the baby's room," Kai said. Becky's step slowed. "I know we said we would wait for whatever shakes out in June, but what's the point in living in fear of the apocalypse? I think our life has waited enough."

That could mean many things, not the least of which was the time that had passed while they hoped for the perfect adoption. Or the years she had wasted, distracted over Brian—not just his research. She had only recently made the admission to herself, and it still stung. For so long, she had thought Kai was the distracted one, but it turned out he had been responding to her. Their relationship was still fragile with the new revelations, but finally they were together in their imperfection.

She squeezed his hand and laid her head on his arm. They walked a few yards then she stepped in front of him. She ran her hands along his shoulders, broader than she ever realized, and she kissed him like they were back in Hawaii. He responded by picking her up as though she were no heavier than Muon, and he carried her into their own house, their own life.

44

March 26: 76%

The Tuesday after Dennis Greeley's wedding, Aiyana drove to Becky and Kai's house for dinner. It was bound to be awkward, but she had no excuse to refuse. When she arrived, Kai met her at the door. "Come on in. Becky's in the living room. Would you like a drink?"

She said yes then found Becky on the couch reading a magazine. "Oh, I thought I heard the doorbell. I'm so glad you're here. How's work?"

Aiyana said work was fine and asked how the students were doing, to which Becky responded that they were fine. Kai returned and handed Aiyana a glass then sat next to Becky. She smiled up at him, and he draped an arm around the back of the couch.

They chatted about their day, as though nothing had ever happened, nor was about to happen. When the stove buzzer sounded, they all got up and went to the dining room. Instead of the usual mounds of crafts, the table was covered with beautiful place settings, a gift from Kai's parents that Becky had always been reluctant to use. She brought in several serving dishes.

"Smells delicious," Kai said, and it did.

"Bourbon-glazed salmon with rice pilaf and broccoli salad? My favorites," Aiyana said.

Becky smiled. "Yes, and fried apple pie for dessert." Also Aiyana's favorite.

When Becky had said the blessing, and they had all been served, and Kai had filled the water glasses, and they were starting a second round of pass-the-pepper, Aiyana couldn't stand it any more. "Okay, what's going on?"

Becky looked at Kai, who shrugged. She took a deep breath. "We have something to ask you."

She could not imagine what it might be, at least not anything she thought they knew about.

"We want to you be our child's godmother."

Aiyana almost choked on her pilaf. "You're kidding." She glanced back and forth between them, but Becky's face was as earnest as ever, and Kai had an expression of it-wasn't-my-idea. She said, "You're talking a fairy godmother, right, like getting her ready for fancy dress balls and buying glass shoes and things? Because I might be able to handle that."

"No, more like a guardian in case something should happen to us. And a…spiritual sounding board."

"Becky, don't be stupid. I'm an atheist." Aiyana went back to eating her salmon.

Kai's face said I-told-you-so. Becky persisted. "I know you and I interpret the world differently, but because of that, I have learned there is far more to the universe than any one person can ever fully understand. It has made me appreciate God even more. It has also made me a better teacher because I'm open to uncertainty now. It's kind of counter-intuitive, but sometimes showing my kids I don't know every answer actually empowers them to be curious. We learn together. I want that for my daughter. My mother's mind is like both fists closed so tightly around what she believes that there isn't room in her grasp for doubt. But I'm trying to do better, to hold my Christianity in one hand and reach beyond religion with the other."

Aiyana wiped her mouth with a corner of her napkin. "Becky, I appreciate the thought, but let's be honest. When it comes to religion, I'm probably not the most open-minded person you know."

"That's okay; we're going to raise her with a Christian foundation. I just want her to have someone to talk to who thinks differently but won't cut her down for raising questions. Someone who cares enough about her to have the conversation. I want to give her the opportunity to look beyond what she knows because it is in seeking that God is found."

Oh, hell. Aiyana didn't want to lead anyone toward the fallacy of God. She was glad to find out their conversations made a difference—but a guardian? Aiyana knew nothing about kids. "Becky, I'll have to think about it."

Becky opened her mouth to speak, but Kai put a hand over hers. "She needs time. She's stubborn, remember?"

Aiyana smirked.

After dinner, they moved onto the deck with their dessert. Soon, Kai excused himself to go back to work. He kissed Becky on the top of her head and went inside.

"He has three new clients," Becky explained after he left. "He doesn't need Brian's research to succeed." She positively oozed pride.

The turnaround was remarkable compared to their relationship less than a month before. Aiyana said, "Can you please explain to me what's happening right now?"

Becky laughed and offered her a cup of tea.

"Really, Becky. I can't remember the last time I visited when Kai was even here, let alone having dinner with us and chatting about the universe over apple pie."

"That's true." Becky set the teapot on its tray and leaned back against the wooden bench. "He's been the invisible man all these years."

"Because he was keeping secrets from you." Aiyana leaned forward to see Becky clearly. The moon hid behind a screen of clouds, creating a dim gray light and deep shadows across the edge of the deck.

"No, because I never asked. So he supported the thing I paid attention to. He supported Brian."

"Doesn't it bother you how he used Brian's research?"

"When a cucumber rolls to the back of the fridge and gets forgotten, it rots. That's what happens to people, too, when no one cares enough to notice."

Aiyana shook her head and sat back hard in her deck chair. She couldn't believe her ears. "You're saying it's not his fault."

"I'm saying that if I had cleaned out the fridge, the cucumber wouldn't have rotted. And if Kai hadn't valued Brian's research when no one else did, Brian would have been the cucumber."

Becky and her analogies. "Have you talked to Brian since we came back?"

"No. We've sacrificed as much as we're going to for him."

Aiyana was surprised at the steely edge in Becky's voice. Was that how couples managed? Sharing their darkest secrets then burying the evidence and pretending it never existed? That's what the Greeleys had done. And Brian had been at the center of Kai and Becky's relationship since the moment they met. Could they suddenly cut him out and carry on? Was that what she had done with Dmitri? Aiyana breathed in the stagnant air. If only it would rain.

She changed the subject, but her mind stayed on Dmitri for the rest of the evening. During her drive home, she remembered something she had tried to forget. Dmitri was not just declared insane; he was first declared incompetent. The word made her shudder. One of the court doctors said he had mental trauma but that he would come out of it in time to stand trial. Another was convinced that he was perfectly competent and choosing not to speak out of insolence. After six months, neither of them could prove either theory, and Dmitri was involuntarily committed. Aiyana couldn't imagine anything more horrible. His condition hadn't changed in nine years, so there he lingered, east of campus, west of the orphanage, and a long way from Siberia.

Aiyana shook her head and repeated what she had told herself for years. The guy was clearly insane, he was where he belonged, and there was nothing she could do. Another consideration pushed to the front of her mind. Maybe Becky wasn't wearing rose-colored glasses and Brian wasn't burying his head in the sand; maybe they were also trying to accept the truth, that what's done is done, what's going to happen will happen, and if you can't change it, there is no point in dwelling on it.

Aiyana's perspective had vacillated over the past few weeks, but in the times when she admitted her powerlessness, her mind was calm. She felt that stillness again as she pulled into a parking spot and turned off the car. Her silly little cards hadn't saved the campus and kept a criminal from becoming; Dennis Greeley had chosen to get help. That choice had come from inside himself, not from Aiyana. She hadn't submitted those case studies for publication because deep down, she thought her little energy beam was a mere placebo; her patients had saved themselves. The ones with the good attitude and the belief in prayer and the desire to be healthy were the ones who responded best. She had looked them in the eyes and claimed to have the power to heal, but her only power was in saying the words that triggered their internal restoration.

It was refreshing to let go of the constant sense of responsibility, the weight of ills, the struggle of knowing what to do, and the guilt of not doing enough. She felt light-headed all of a sudden, so she was glad to be home.

She breathed deeply as she walked down the street toward her brownstone. The air was still stagnant, but the muted moon glow was enough to lead her to the doorstep. A shadow sat at the top, waiting for her. It was Brian.

45

March 26: 77%

"You look like crap," Aiyana told Brian. His sweatshirt hung from his body like a washcloth on a wire rack, and his eyes were set in dark caves on his ashen face. "You need a peanut butter sandwich or something." He stood up from the step, and she moved past him to unlock the door.

"Did you feel the earthquake?" he asked.

"What?"

"The earthquake. Did you feel it?"

"You're not making any sense."

"There was an earthquake."

"Yes, I know that! In Greece. Two weeks ago. I heard it was huge, but I hardly think anyone here would have felt it."

"No, last night. In Oklahoma." His irises glowed like emergency flares. She steered him through the living room and onto a kitchen stool then tossed him a package of trail mix. "There was also a micro quake in Saskatchewan last week and one in Siberia two weeks ago."

"Siberia?" Aiyana took a drink of water. "Brian, why are you here?" She was acutely aware of how odd his presence felt. In her mind, he had lived in the lab; her mental images did not include him having a home or sitting at her breakfast nook eating sunflower seeds and peanuts. She might as well have been feeding kibble to a black-backed jackal sprung from the zoo.

"Seismic waves. That's how acoustic energy travels through the earth after a quake."

"You can't be suggesting that earthquakes in Siberia, Canada, and Oklahoma are related to the one in Greece."

"They could be. Seismic waves after a major earthquake can trigger minor earthquakes in areas with tectonic stress halfway across the world."

She sat on the stool next to him and straightened the disheveled pile of papers he had brought. The papers contained updated models of Freedom, Kansas, and similar models from Boston to Baja and British Columbia to Belize.

"What if the energy we're measuring travels in waves through people like seismic waves travel through the earth? We've been studying patterns of data points over time to predict violence in other areas, not only Freedom, and we've identified nearly a hundred epicenters in North and South America. So there could be a thousand across the world. What if they're all connected?" He grabbed the papers and frantically shuffled through them. "I spent the whole night drafting a model of the data between epicenters in the likely scenario that major violence hits Freedom in eight weeks." He shoved a map in her direction. It was peppered with large red circles like targets on each continent.

"Brian, I don't know what I'm looking at. Why—"

"It's a world war."

She stumbled back, her mouth agape.

"Aiyana, don't think that. I'm not crazy."

Brian rose from his stool and took a step toward Aiyana, but she slid along the counter and grabbed her phone. He said, "Call Kai. He'll believe me."

"Yes, I'll call Kai." She dialed, and Becky answered. "Get Kai on the phone."

Aiyana and Brian stared at each other intently, until Kai and Becky both joined the other end of the line. "Brian came for a visit," Aiyana said.

"What? Is he alright?"

"I don't think so."

Without explaining, she readily agreed to drive him back to their place for the night.

As Brian followed Aiyana to the car, they didn't speak. The dense clouds fully obscured the moon, and the darkness closed in on the streetlight while it glowed a weak final protest. They drove in silence along the residential streets until Aiyana said, "It's one scenario. The worst case."

"It's the most likely case."

"What's most likely? Sixty percent? Seventy? That still leaves thirty or forty percent for some other scenario."

"Are you willing to take that chance?"

Aiyana's hands started to shake, and she gripped the wheel tightly. "There is already violence all over the world."

"Not of this magnitude."

She turned onto Main Street, and they drove through town. There was little activity in the late hour except for a pocket of teenagers looking for trouble and a man sitting on the street curb with no place to go.

"How can Freedom, Kansas possibly be the source?"

"It's the epicenter of all epicenters. It's within one degree latitude of the central point of the United States and one degree longitude of the central point of North America. It's on the border between two states. At noontime, Becky's house casts a shadow on Nebraska but never casts one on Kansas. It's a geographical convergence point."

His intensity made the connections seem momentous, but they were merely coincidence. "Brian, look at history. When has anything in Kansas made a difference to the world?"

"The Kansas-Nebraska Act of the 1800s triggered a series of events that precipitated the U.S. Civil War. That had reverberations across North America and Europe."

Aiyana jerked the steering wheel and sped onto the rural route out of town. "That was about the entire institution of slavery, not a domestic dispute, and Kansas wasn't the only place that turned bloody over it."

"But if Kansas hadn't been involved, or if one of the other bloody micro-wars had never happened, the tide of history might have changed."

They flew along Route 36, paralleled on either side by miles of fields punctuated every few minutes by a farmhouse.

"This is all fascinating, but Freedom is in nowhere land. There are barely enough people to spread the news, so I don't expect anyone in Kansas City to care about what happens here, let alone anyone in Denver or St. Louis, and forget New York or Los Angeles."

"It's precisely because of the sparse population that the event, whatever it is, will be the focal topic; no bigger news will exist to detract from the story. The city papers across the nation will pick it up because it strikes at the core of the country, not only geographically but symbolically. If our very heartland can suffer large-scale violence, then how can safety exist anywhere? The event will shatter any lingering myth confining daily violence to urban war zones, and the problem will loom too large to see past. Hopelessness will be the kindling, and Freedom will be the microcosm of frustration and despair that will spread from the U.S. across the Americas, and from the Americas to other continents, and eventually the entire world."

In front of Becky's house, Aiyana jammed the car into park. "You make it sound like we're gearing up for the ultimate battle of good versus evil. Except life is not a comic book, and you're no superhero." She got out of the car and slammed the door. "We're here!" she hollered. Becky and Kai came out to the porch, the backwoods blonde and the third-generation immigrant standing out like the new Americana.

They pretended not to notice Brian's gaunt appearance as they all went into the house. The kitchen smelled like fresh-baked cookies. Good old Becky. She gave two to Brian.

"What's going on?" Kai asked, the first one to speak.

"We're not going to talk about it tonight," Becky said. She pressed a cup of warm milk into Brian's hand. "It's after midnight. We're going to sleep and talk about it tomorrow."

"I have to work tomorrow," Aiyana said, not eager to continue the conversation.

"I do, too," Becky said. "So, tomorrow night." She hesitated as she looked at Brian, who was gingerly holding his milk and cookies in the homey light of the kitchen. Becky turned to Kai. "Will you…?"

"Yes," he sighed. "I'll stay here tomorrow."

None of them expected to sleep that night, but they did. The sun rose the next day as always, and Aiyana got up before anyone else to go back home and get ready for work. She was greeted by her receptionist when she arrived, a little later than usual. "Doctor Rivers, there's a situation." Aiyana followed the receptionist to the back of the clinic where a crowd was gathering on the sidewalk.

A man in a blood-stained white-collared shirt was holding his nose and glaring in the direction of a woman in sweatpants. The woman was saying, "Every morning when I drop off my son at school, there's somebody on their cell phone or not using their blinker or otherwise acting like they're the only driver on the road. Then today, I almost hit a dog trying to avoid this guy's truck because he was doing it all and then some. It scared me. I don't know; I guess I hit my limit."

"You punched him?" asked an incredulous pre-teen. "Awesome!"

The man shook his head in disgust then flinched in pain. The woman smiled oddly. "Yes, but I feel better now."

Aiyana brought the man into the clinic, stuffed him with a couple of nasal packs, and let him go. She gave the woman a quick examination, but there were no injuries. In fact, she told Aiyana, she hadn't felt so good in weeks.

A month earlier, Aiyana would have interpreted the incident as a sign of doom, of the prediction coming true, of the rise of entropy. A month earlier, Brian seemed perfectly sane, a brilliant scientist.

She dismissed the incident as a harmless escape of steam. It lowered some pressure, the man had deserved it, and the woman would be fine. She wouldn't run him over or kick her dog—or her kids—in some needless act of desperation. Wars didn't happen because of anything that went on in a small town like Freedom. No event within ten square miles was going to cause the meltdown of humanity.

At Freedom High School, Becky watched the kids file through the loathsome metal detector and into the lunchroom to await their first class of the day. A group of boys shoved each other back and forth as they made their way down the hall, kidding around as usual. A group of girls congregated around a locker, whispering, their eyes wide with a juicy secret. They appeared to be normal, boisterous, fun-loving teenagers.

But Becky could see beyond the surface. Their auras used to be wide and intermingled and full of color, but the flickers had become dim and narrow and were held so close they didn't connect anymore. Their laughter was hollow, and there was no inclination of the eagerness and hopeful visions of the future that a young person should be able to feel about the world.

Why should there be? They were teenagers, full of responsibility without control. Waiting on the adults to get their acts together and fix the world. But they weren't stupid. They could read in the news and observe in their own community that togetherness was a long way from happening. Yet what could they do about it? So much, Becky thought. Kids were capable of amazing things when given the opportunity.

The bell rang, and the students headed to their first classes. After a few minutes, the hall cleared out, and Becky saw a pregnant girl walking slowly from the nurse's office toward the Home Economics room. Even she, the guidance counselor's stepdaughter, hadn't seen the bright future before her—at least not enough to protect it. Becky remembered when the girl's family had first moved to town, she immediately became popular, her white glow large and focal. Today she walked alone in the hall, hugging her books closely to her bulging stomach, pulled tight like her gray aura.

Becky's curiosity got the better of her, and she followed the girl to the childcare class. She slowed as she walked past the door and glanced at the four girls inside. Their baggy clothes disguised how far along they were in their pregnancy. Becky shook her head. No, the mother of her baby—whether she was one of those girls or someone else—didn't want her identity known. Yet Becky watched the four of them and wondered how much of a child's character was determined by genes versus parenting and circumstance and peers. She wished she had the data to understand the combinations and figure out the triggers she could control.

She turned around to go back to her classroom. She heard two boys behind her say, "Hey, when you're done with that bun, I know where you can get another one!"

The Home Ec teacher said, "Get on to your own class!" and the door slammed.

Kids had great potential, but they could be merciless, too. Becky cut past the band room to get back to the freshman wing. She overheard two students among the squeak and strum of practice for an upcoming guitar exam.

"Okay, play a G chord." Strum. "No, that's C."

"Yeah, 'cause C comes first."

"What the hell? When the teacher asks for a G chord, you play a frickin' G chord. You can't choose! No wonder you're failing."

Becky held back a smile. When she got to her classroom and shut the door, the interchange crossed her mind again, and she started to laugh. The kids looked around, surprised and perplexed. Becky took a deep breath, but it set her off again, and a ripple of giggles spread across the room. Then a student laughed out loud, like it was church and couldn't be helped. Several others followed, including Becky. She took another breath and waved her hands to settle the room, letting loose a few last chuckles as she told them the objectives for the day. When everyone was calm again, one student asked her what was so funny.

"I don't know, I guess I just felt like laughing."

They started the period by reviewing the students' research on record-breaking weather events of the last century. Halfway through class, they arranged their desks in a circle and role-played different scientists, arguing about global warming and whether or not it was due mainly to burning oil and coal. The discussion deviated to the comments below the online articles they had found, and one student asked why people had to be cruel about it. "Because it's important!" another shot back. Several other students joined in, and the heat rose in all of their faces. Becky knew such strong reactions couldn't be merely about climate change, so she stopped the conversation and gave them an opportunity to explain—rationally and one at a time—about their experiences with reading the comments.

At first, they tossed out descriptors like "pointless", "helpless", and "mean". Then a girl who was friends with one of the pregnant teens explained, "It's like when people say bad things about your friends online. You get frustrated because you can't do anything about it. If you tell them it's not right, they just spit another rotten thing back at you."

The girl next to her said, "Yeah, and half the time people use fake names. They don't dare to say stuff like that to your face."

The rest of the students picked up on the theme, bouncing their thoughts around the circle and nodding their heads at chords of truth.

"Some of those comments go back and forth for like, fifty pages. Even if they're strangers. Doesn't anybody realize you can't talk a person out of hating you for no reason?"

"I don't want to read it, but I can't help it. It's weird. I can spend a whole hour caught right up in it and not even realize until after."

"Me, too! Then I'm in a bad mood the rest of the night."

One of Becky's more troublesome students said, "It's like when you're late for school or somethin' and the hundred-year-old q-tip in front of you is on a Sunday drive and you need to get there, but she won't step on the gas, and you can't get around her, so all you can do is lay on the horn and cuss." He gestured in demonstration, and a dragon tattoo flamed out beneath the wrist of his shirt. The principal had told him a hundred times to cover it, but it refused to be hidden.

Becky left the floor open for one more comment, and a boy who often reminded her of Brian said, "I don't know what you guys are talking about. I just read enough to get the assignment done then go have a life."

Becky summarized it a little more diplomatically as stepping away from what the world is shouting so they could hear what was valuable inside their own minds. They turned back to the climate discussion for another twenty minutes until Becky said, "Okay, it sounds like there are arguments on both sides, and maybe more information is available for one side than the other. What I want you to do before you leave is to write down at least two *predictions* that most of the scientists agree upon, even if they don't agree on the *cause*."

They scribbled silently for a few minutes until the sounds of ripping notebook pages mixed with the end-of-class bell. Becky stood at the door, collecting the students' answers as they left. She glanced through them, expecting to see one or two smart-alec remarks per usual, but was surprised to read serious answers from all of them: *Temperature of the earth will increase. Glaciers will melt. Seas will get higher. Weather patterns will change.*

She heard one student say to another, "I don't know what I'm supposed to believe, but there's some scary shit going on in the world."

The other replied, "Yeah, and like recycling my water bottle is really going to make a difference."

That evening, Becky decided to stay in the living room while Brian explained his new theories. She didn't want any part of it, but she couldn't help hearing Brian's feverish explanations, punctuated by Aiyana's insistence that he was crazy, followed by a rehash of why their brainstorming weekend at New Tech proved that doing nothing was their only option. Kai's voice was too low to hear. Becky didn't want to know what he was saying, anyway.

She flipped through the exit tickets from her classes to figure out what she needed to tweak in the next day's lesson plan. She was pleased that all of her students came up with two answers, except for her first class of the day, where every student came up with three or four. Becky leaned back into the couch and ruffled Muon's fur as she wondered what to make of those results. Maybe they were meaningless. She picked up the cat and hugged him tightly until he struggled against her. Then she kissed him between the ears and said, "Resistance is futile," and let him go. He ran to the scratching post and picked out his irritation, raining fibers onto the floor. An oblivious Neutrino walked by, and Muon pounced. They wrestled for a couple of minutes, equally matched, then licked each other and walked away.

Brian was saying, "Acts of violence move in waves, and waves can multiply or divide. In the ocean, two waves mix together and swell if they're in phase. I'm telling you, all of the epicenters we've measured have a 60% overlap in phase with adjacent areas. That means when the repercussions start to spread, the violence is likely to swell to a tidal wave. Or worse."

"What do you mean by 'likely'?" Aiyana said. "There's a good probability that nothing will happen at all."

"I'm not talking about probabilities. But say I was. It's not so much a question of happening or not happening; it's an issue of magnitude. When the weatherman forecasts a 60% chance of rain, I grab an umbrella. When he says there is a 60% chance that four of the biggest storms crossing the ocean are going to meet in my county and create devastation like nothing ever seen before, I evacuate."

"Fine, then," Aiyana said. "Tell people. Let's take the data to the mayor and ask him to evacuate." No one answered. Aiyana went on. "If this were a hurricane, we could put it on a map and show it moving, and people could see the pictures of the devastation to homes, battered shorelines, downed trees, a death toll. You could show it to them every hour on the hour and say with confidence that the storm going to land here at 11:00 AM on Tuesday, so people should go somewhere else. But what you're talking about is uncertain at best, and there is no precedent. At least not one we can prove. This Franken-storm is in the mind, so there's no way to evacuate. Even—"

Brian cut her off. "Waves can also cancel each other out. When they meet up at different phases, they swirl down in randomness. So while we might not be able to prevent the wave of violence in Freedom, if we could dampen it or delay it or somehow shift it, we could at least reduce the risk of it spreading somewhere else."

"How? Even if I believed you, we'd be right where we were a month ago, with no feasible ideas."

"Cloud seeding," Kai said, loud enough for Becky to hear. She tensed. "Using ions to make people feel better was always feasible, just not acceptable. Maybe things have changed."

In the long pause that followed, Becky couldn't tell whether they were whispering. Then Aiyana spoke loudly. "Why stop there? Why not lace the water supply with mood-enhancing drugs?"

"Okay," Kai said, "why don't we scale up your energy machines and pass people through them at the mall or something? Like a novelty. We can go to your clinic tomorrow, take a—"

"No, you can't. I shut them down."

That was news to Becky.

"The energy therapy was a placebo, like religion or anything else. If people *want* to feel better, they'll feel better. If not, well, end of story."

A minute later, the front door squeaked open and closed firmly, then the headlights of Aiyana's car shone through the living room window as she drove away.

Brian said, "The ions couldn't help, anyway. Maybe before, when it was only about Freedom…but it's not any more. Drawing the rain here could have a side effect of prolonging drought in other areas and expanding other epicenters, or worse. So we have to look past ourselves to something bigger and consider the chain effect." He dropped his voice, and Becky strained to listen. "Whatever we do has to spread fast. We're running out of time."

46

March 27: 77%

During the drive to school the next day, the conversation wouldn't leave Becky's mind. Everything in her screamed that Aiyana was wrong. Religion was not just a placebo. God was at her core. When her faith was strong, two waves of the same phase swelled inside her.

Sometimes she got out of phase, as when Aiyana stirred up clouds of doubt, or when her mind was pulled like a magnet to Brian while her soul was enduringly with Kai. At those times, her own self inside was flat, but a current remained underneath. It lapped at her heart so softly she could barely feel it, but whenever she quieted her mind, it was there.

She couldn't force Aiyana to believe in a soul any more than she could coax Dmitri to speak or force her students to learn science. She could only create an opening; they had to want to go through it. Unless it was impossible for Aiyana to believe or for a student to learn or for Dmitri to speak—but that was not for Becky to decide.

The first period of the day was an open house. As the students paraded their parents through the halls, showing off their artwork and math lessons, Becky couldn't help thinking about them in light of the victims detailed in Brian's letters.

Would the father in the polo shirt take out his frustration on wife and kids? Would the mother in the canvas shoes and mommy jeans leave her family because she'd had enough? Would one of their children commit suicide? Would any of them succumb to an instant of desperation that could change the course of a life: assault, robbery, overdose? Which came first, the crime or the fear?

During the second period, Dillon sat in the back, unengaged. Becky didn't know what was going on with him, but she was afraid to look into those pale eyes and see helplessness or anger—and possibly trigger him to do something they both would regret. So when he put his head down on his desk in the middle of class, she let him. Nothing had changed since the day before, but futility wound through all of Becky's thoughts. Teenagers were like Aiyana's patients: if they wanted to learn, they would find a way. If they didn't, how much could a teacher really do?

During lunch duty, she leaned against a wall and watched the students in their cliques with their bag lunches and cafeteria food, talking about who knows what. Suddenly, a table of girls in the center of the room burst into loud laughter. Becky and the rest of the cafeteria tensed in paranoia. Usually an explosion of laughter meant gossip was being spread at someone else's expense, in which case the flame would flash and die. But it continued in belly laughs that renewed at each exhaustion and sparked a couple of boys at the adjacent table to start laughing as well; then the whole table joined in. More students turned to look, and Becky watched as the curiosity transformed to giggles. It didn't affect everyone, but the mirth spread across the cafeteria in bursts of yellow. At the edges of the room, there were only brief smiles, but they were real, and more than she had seen in weeks.

When the commotion eventually petered out, Becky made her way over to the table in the center. "What was so funny?" she asked.

They all shrugged, and one girl answered, "I guess we just felt like laughing."

47

March 27: 78%

Becky rushed from the cafeteria back to her classroom and quickly typed into her computer before the students arrived for their next class. *Is laughter contagious?* The search engine pulled up scientific studies on the spread of laughter. *Is happiness contagious?* Maps of the world showed areas of happiness and equations linking the spread among families and communities. Having a happy friend who lived nearby could make a person up to 25% more likely to be happy herself. Happy friends of friends added to the likelihood.

After school, Becky begged out of her track coaching duties and drove straight to Aiyana's clinic. She told the receptionist who she was, and soon, Aiyana emerged from an exam room, concern all over her face. "Are you okay? What happened?"

Becky said, "Laughter brightens aura!"

Aiyana glanced sharply toward the receptionist and the patient in the waiting room. She put a hand on Becky's shoulder. "Let's go in the back and talk." She guided her into the office and closed the door.

Becky continued excitedly. "The facial muscles that move when we laugh are linked to neurons in the mood areas of the brain. The signal runs both ways! Smiling triggers the neurons, but the neurons also trigger a smile. Either way, it releases stress! Didn't you learn these things in medical school?"

Aiyana said, "I don't...What?" She sat Becky in a chair.

"Kai and Brian said we needed something that would move fast. Well, what goes viral faster than laughter? You said it yourself: people have to want to be happy."

Aiyana squeezed her eyelids together and rubbed her forehead. Becky's words tumbled out as fast as she could think them. "We've been searching for the firewood that *makes* people feel good, but we missed the most important part—the kindling! The stress reliever is laughter itself. There's research to prove it. Smiles are contagious. Happiness is contagious. Laughter is a wave! And it spreads faster than fear. So if we can prime people to laugh, we'll not only cancel out the waves of violence; we'll spread joy. It can work like a rain shower, on the inside!"

Aiyana turned away from her. "You're not making any sense."

"Of course I am. You know I am." Aiyana moved to the other side of the office, trying to put the desk between them, but Becky followed her. "I'm not saying it will be easy, but it's a lot easier than what we've been trying to do. Because it isn't about taking away individual stressors. The bigger issue, the one that creates stress in the first place, is perception. When you read hateful comments or take in bad news for hours on end, your sour mood feeds on itself and colors what you perceive and how you react. You start to see only the negative, and you start to think that this is the extent of the world; I can't change all the hate and ignorance and fear and disrespect, not even in my own community, not even in my own mind. The more helpless you feel, the more you react like a victim and curl in upon yourself. You start to view every person as a predator."

Becky barely paused to take a breath. "But we can trigger our town to look for something better. There is so much more to people than the negative. There is a fire of joy somewhere inside of everyone, and laughter is the kindling, don't you see? We never know what's going to happen next, but uncertainty can be either the root of fear or the cornerstone of hope. It all depends on the observer."

"Becky! Would you stop talking for a *minute*?" Aiyana sat hard in her desk chair and dropped her head in her hands. "Is it me, or is the whole world going nuts?"

"It's you."

Becky left Aiyana alone to sort out her thoughts. She e-mailed her a list of links to the research she had found, with a note: *There is something we can do.*

48

Fear is a fire
In your belly
Beneath your feet

Flee it or fight
Action confined
Chasing, leaping
Embers left behind

Searing, smoke
Clarity, confusion
Apprehension
Love or Hate
Defined by reaction

Life, Force
Indecision
Fear is anxiety
Traveling, consuming

Surprise
Tension
Obstacle
Paralysis

49

March 27: 79%

After Becky's visit, Aiyana finished her next appointment then left all of her wrap-up work in the clinic and went home to think. Two hours later, she sat cross-legged on the hardwood floor with her back to the sliding glass and a pad of paper in her hand. On it, she had written:

I thought I should change the world.

I thought I would change the world.

I thought I could change the world.

But it turns out, I'm not strong enough. Not nearly.

Part of her wanted to believe that Becky and Brian were right, that they could shift the phase of the impending wave of violence to keep it from spreading beyond Freedom. She wanted to believe that they could save people from destroying themselves. Still, a part of her didn't think such a thing was possible, not in big ways, but especially not in a way so small and simple as a perspective or a laugh—something a mere baby could do. Another part of her was afraid to try. If her pessimism were confirmed, and her illusions of power and control and yes, destiny, were taken away, who would she be?

She leaned her head back against the door and thought of some of the people who had changed centuries of science and medicine: Einstein, Newton, Darwin, Eisenberg, Pasteur, Curie, Schrödinger, Crick, Watson, Fermi, Feynman, and Gauss. She should be one of those people. She had the pieces: the intelligence, the drive, the presence. Yet her reach was limited, and the world kept getting bigger and more out of control. How could any one person in the present be as important as those giants of history?

She wondered if the giants were even so big themselves. They had built their theories upon those that came before, and they must have had support from a colleague or a friend. Maybe history remembers those who published their data when the right people are ready to use it. Maybe previous pioneers had made the same momentous discoveries, but they were marginalized in their time.

The smallest part of her wrote an admission on the notepad: *I want the credit.* She looked at the sentence, so petty on the page. But it was the truth. She didn't want to think that the tide of history could be changed by a collection of everyday actions. She wanted it to need an act so monumental that the four of them would have to be acknowledged for bearing the risk and be held up as heroes. She didn't want to be forgotten.

She shook off the admission and got up from the floor. Either she believed or she didn't. She had to choose and move forward.

50

March 31: 80%

Aiyana, Becky, Brian, and Kai were finally in agreement: they should do something, and theoretically, there was something they could do. They still had no idea what the something would be, but knowing they were all working toward a common goal, Aiyana felt lighter somehow. The others seemed to feel it too as they gathered on the deck for a Sunday evening cookout.

Kai flipped a burger in the air toward Brian. Brian didn't react quickly enough, and the patty landed on the bench beside him. Kai said, "You still have to eat that."

"Yeah, yeah, cows don't grow on trees," Brian said.

Aiyana couldn't believe the change in him in the short week he'd been staying with Becky and Kai. He was obviously being fed well, and he looked almost like the same old Brian, with a few more wrinkles. He still broke into his mad scientist intensity when showing them the latest probabilities, which had only increased since they had begun the discussion. The whole situation was surreal: facing down Armageddon, the long-suffering love triangle living under the same roof, and a brainstorming picnic at sunset.

The evening had started out as a business meeting. Aiyana and Becky had shared the laughter research, and they had decided to host an event that would serve as a spark. The event had two principles: 1) people would show up, and 2) people would laugh.

That's where they got stuck.

The problem wasn't merely the logistics of an event for ten thousand people. It wasn't coming up with assumptions for Brian's model. It wasn't even the difficulty of creating an experience with wide enough appeal to meet their outcome goals, although the challenge was daunting. The main problem was that they had forgotten how to be happy themselves. Laughter had been reduced to criteria and variables and the solution to a life-altering problem. That's when they decided to move outside and try to set themselves free from the gravity.

"What would make you show up?" Becky asked to no one in particular as she squirted mustard on her burger. The question was met by silence. Regardless of what the event was, three of the four of them probably wouldn't attend if they weren't the ones throwing it. Becky said, "Well, I wouldn't go to any slapstick marathon."

"What?" Kai said. "What about bad scary movies?"

"No, I like my humor with a little brain, thank you."

Brian said, "I like spoof music, especially when there's fiddles."

Kai tossed Aiyana an ear of corn. She caught it, perplexed by the conversation.

"What do you want, Aiyana? Something a little more high brow, perhaps?" Kai assumed a fake British accent.

"Actually," she said, "I always laughed in church, when I wasn't supposed to." She was genuinely amused by the childhood memory.

"Okay, Aiyana can run the no smiling zone," Becky said.

"We could make it a competition. What's a festival without a competition?" Kai said.

"We could call it the World Poker Face Tournament." Aiyana tossed out the stupid thought in the spirit of being free.

Brian gave her a high five. "Heck, why do any of this? Why not just play reels of people laughing? It's contagious, right Becky?"

"Sure, we'll drive around blasting the world's most contagious laugh all day. That's bound to make people feel good."

"Okay, and let's include cats. Lots and lots of crazy cats."

The festival planning devolved into yet sillier ideas bounced back and forth among the four while they laughed like drunk monkeys. Becky said, "Stop! My sides hurt!" as she held her stomach and doubled over.

"Maybe you should have built up your muscles with laughter yoga before we started!" That brought on gales more chortling. Not because it was funny, but because they had succeeded in letting loose their control.

Around ten o'clock, Brian said, "I feel like running." He jumped up from his seat, saying to Kai, "I'll race you." The two men ran across the yard to the field. Brian, out of shape, was far behind when they reached the cornfield, and he fell over to the ground in exaggerated concession. Kai dropped down where he was and lay sprawled on the lawn. Becky and Aiyana could hear their groans floating on the wind toward them.

"Who needs a puppy when you have a husband?"

On Monday morning, the neighbors across the field called Becky and thanked her and Kai for checking on the house while they were gone. "We heard you folks out there last night. Sounded like a good time." They chatted a few minutes until Becky had to excuse herself to go to school for an early morning staff meeting.

Becky slipped in a few minutes late to a seat in the back of the library, where the meeting was already in progress. The topic being discussed was the recent advent of disruptive laughter among the students.

"They're bursting out in the middle of class, and every student is part of it."

"There's no way to maintain control in this environment."

"The more I try to impose discipline, the more they laugh. It's infuriating."

Becky listened to their consternation, feeling a bit guilty for having encouraged it. But the angrier they became, the more justified she felt. Finally, she spoke up. "Has it occurred to you that these kids are relieving stress, and we should let them?" At least twenty pairs of eyes, including the principal's, turned to her in amazement. "I don't try to stop it any more. I build laughter time into my lesson plan, and as it turns out, the learning is better."

The principal scolded her. "There is no place for that kind of behavior in a school."

Becky's eyebrows flew up in outrage, although everyone around her was nodding. "No place for fun in a building full of kids?"

"They're not kids, they're teenagers."

Becky let out a snort. She gathered her notebook, pen, and purse, and stood up to leave, continuing to sniggle while the other teachers stared. At the door, she stopped and said, "If you can't beat 'em, join 'em."

Throughout the morning, she felt camaraderie with her students, all of them subjects of a subtle tyranny. She hadn't become a teacher to guard a prison. "Teenagers" weren't something to be carried out between two fingers; they were kids. And they were under her care. *Care.*

She also noticed that the kids had more solidarity and confidence than they had displayed in months. Not everyone, though. Dillon came in and immediately put his head on the desk. He was past the point of help, but if anyone else in town had low spirits that could be lifted before reaching such a state, Becky vowed to do her best to lift them.

That night, the four friends met at Kai's office downtown, where Brian had set up a makeshift workstation in an empty office. The three secretaries had gone home, and Kai's eight consultants who were based in Freedom were all out working with new clients. Becky didn't come to his office frequently, but each time she did, she was amazed at how Kai could run a multi-million dollar operation with so few employees—or at least so few that she could see. When she had asked him about it, he told her the key to being responsive to his clients was having a roster of trusted specialists whom he could mobilize by contract to match skills to needs, rather than carrying generalists on a permanent payroll. His office space was state-of-the-art but sparse. There was very little flurry because when Kai did hire people, he was able to screen them for their desire to actually be productive over merely looking busy.

They gathered in the conference room to read the week's results. The probability of a catastrophic event in Freedom was holding steady at 80%. However, there had been a sharp increase over the previous week in the phase alignment with other areas. So anything that happened in Freedom was increasingly likely to have far-reaching consequences.

They had planned to do more strategizing, but Becky started the discussion by saying, "Why don't we do the festival we talked about? I know we weren't serious, but it was fun, and in hours of brainstorming, we've never thought of anything better." Before the others could object, she rushed ahead. "We can pick a date, and Aiyana, you can invite your patients, and I can invite my church friends and people from school, and we can start advertising then go from there based on the response. What can it hurt?"

In the light of day, the festival was even more of a joke than the night before. But they were running out of time. So, the team grabbed onto the Hail Mary pass and put their full effort into it.

51

All over Freedom, commercials popped up between talk shows and the news and prime time TV. "What was that?" people said to themselves and each other after watching thirty seconds of laughter spreading across subway cars, grocery story lines, and street corners. Each video was followed by a date and a caption: *Laughter is Contagious.*

Flyers showed up in area newspapers:

Have you ever laughed so hard your stomach hurt?
Maybe you need laughter calisthenics.

Do you know there are 30 muscles in the human face, and
it takes 12 of them to make a genuine smile?
If your muscles need conditioning, join us for a smile workout.

Get ready for the Festival of Laughter.
Don't be caught out of shape.

Becky personally invited church members, fellow teachers, administrators, and every parent she had ever talked to, including some she hadn't. Aiyana passed out invitations and a schedule of events to her incredulous staff members and patients.

> Our town needs a good laugh.
> So please come to the Festival and invite your friends.
> Admission is free and the food is, too!
> Sponsored by LaughterIsContagious.org.

The website contained one sentence in the About Us section: *We are just a group of people who want to see you laugh.* The home page contained streaming videos accompanied by links to happiness studies and explanations of the neuroscience behind a smile. One page solicited audio entries and votes for the most contagious laugh contest. A banner of candid photos ran across the top of the site, advertising the Festival of Laughter.

52

A week before the festival, Aiyana was walking down Main Street when a woman stepped out of an alcove and headed toward her. The woman's brows were rising and falling, and her mouth twitched on one side while her eyes stared forward, intense and unseeing. Aiyana slowed as she approached, trying to diagnose the ailment. The woman blinked and shook her head when she noticed Aiyana. The twitching stopped, and she pressed her lips together sheepishly. Aiyana returned a half-smile, confused until she realized they were outside the new laughter gym. She chuckled, and the woman let loose a full-on grin. Aiyana felt herself doing the same. The woman pointed up at the studio sign, and Aiyana nodded in understanding.

Several other joyful people emerged from the alcove, and Aiyana stepped aside to let them pass, then she decided to go in. She ducked down the narrow hallway past the first room where the laughter calisthenics were under way. The ripples of giggles spilled into the hall. She stopped at the second room to observe the smile workout. About thirty people of various ages and a combination of men and women were all sitting on cushioned chairs and holding mirrors. Aiyana was surprised at the cross-section of people. Although the team had tried hard to design classes that would appeal to serious and silly alike, she hadn't been sure they succeeded.

The two experts Kai had hired were beginning a new session. One of the leaders was a physical therapist who specialized in facial muscle retraining for stroke, Bell's Palsy, and dystonia patients; and the other was a retired professor whose brain research focused on frontal cortex involvement in mood disorders. Aiyana stood in the shadow of the doorway to listen.

The professor showed a series of pictures and instructed the attendees to raise their hands at each fake smile. At the end, he asked how they knew, and the class overwhelming credited the eyes. "A genuine smile is called a Duchenne smile", he explained, "named after the man who discovered that a smile involving the eyes makes not only a happy face but a happy brain as well." He told them about a theory that claims the muscles around the eyes are linked to the mood centers in the brain, so not only do people smile when they are happy, but the very act of smiling makes a person feel good. He showed them data in support.

At that point, the physical therapist jumped in. "Let's find out how good you are at *creating* a Duchenne smile." She first had the class hold pencils in their teeth and say "eee". "Don't laugh," she told them, with mock sternness. "This is a non-Duchenne smile. You only need your mouth muscles to do this one. Anybody having trouble with it?" She scanned the room as the participants shook their heads and spat out their pencils; then she told them to hold up their mirrors and try to create a smile only around their eyes. "Do you feel your temple muscles pulling back and your eyebrows pulling up? It's difficult to keep your mouth from going too, isn't it?" After they practiced for a minute, she had them alternate between neutral and smiling eyes. "Your ears are wiggling," she said to one of the students. After a few more minutes, she said, "Okay, let's do a full Duchenne, putting the eyes and mouth together." She told them to pick a partner and watch each other.

The students did as they were told until the therapist directed them to look toward the screen. They chuckled when they saw themselves recorded in a video as they prepared for the exercises. They watched each of the teams break into smiles. The professor said, "Do you notice anything interesting? The partners all smiled back! It's hard to resist a Duchenne smile; we're hard-wired to respond."

While the therapist led the class through a facial massage, Aiyana slipped out. She hadn't sat through a full session since the team had participated in the trial run. Although she was conscious not to practice in public—the incident with the lady on the street confirmed why—after that first session, she and Becky and Kai and Brian had practiced over spaghetti, in the name of due diligence. Aiyana had to admit that it was weird, but it felt good.

She stopped outside to watch the laughter calisthenics class. The building Kai had rented was an old storefront, so the group of twenty or so was on full display in the picture window, with mouths open in uproar like a silent comedy. Anyone who stopped to watch, however, did so at his own peril. Because the leader often put spectators under observation, directing the class to turn and wave them in.

Sometimes the observees complied, and sometimes they hurried on, in case the crazy was contagious.

Aiyana hid herself in the shadow of the alcove. The instructor was barefoot and dressed in a purple tunic with linen pants. He was imported from California and certified in Laughter Yoga®. Aiyana thought the certification was a joke, but Becky had read the research and learned that simulated laughter, generated without comedy or humor, could affect the brain in the same way as real laughter. Laughter Yoga® included eye contact and breathing techniques that could make even simulated laughter become infectious and spontaneous. Becky thought the techniques were worth a try. Brian and Aiyana had reluctantly agreed, although it didn't much matter; the decisions were all up to Kai in the end because he was funding the entire festival.

53

The day of the festival was overcast, which was no surprise. The weather had been that way for months, with the sun a mere memory behind the haze. The empty field-turned-parking lot contained various shades of beige, and last year's grass crinkled under Becky's feet as she made her way through the crowd to survey the festivities.

She saw Kai and waved. He navigated through a group of families to reach her. "Kai!" she exclaimed as he whirled her around in a hug.

"Can you believe how many people are here?" he said.

She shook her head as they surveyed the thousands of participants traveling in clouds of laughter from stage to stage and tent to tent. She squeezed his hand. "You made this happen."

"We all did."

She looked him squarely in the eye. "You negotiated the vendors and rented this farm and got the permits and took care of all of the contracts and a million other business details that the rest of us never would have thought of." She reached up and kissed him on the cheek. "I'm so proud of you." Their mutual gaze lingered until he slid his arm around her waist and pulled her close.

Before they could kiss too long, a voice behind Kai said, "Get a room." Brian was walking toward them and flashing his signature smile, rarely shown since college. For a moment, they were transported back to freshman orientation and a campus full of excitement and possibility. "Have you two heard the comedian at Stage Four, yet? The guy is a riot. I almost wet myself."

They checked their programs and compared notes on the day so far. They had vetted and approved all of the on-stage talent and gained rights to the crazy cat reels and other you-can't-help-smiling-at-this videos playing in the tents, but the experience was different shared with strangers. The reactions were as much as they could have hoped for. The kids were enjoying themselves in time-tested favorites like the world's longest conga line that snaked its way around the edge of the festival and through the families-only field. They were surprised at how the simplest ideas like the "grown-ups only" sprinkler and slide were generating buzz as some of the best events. Apparently, feeling like a kid again was better than just a cliché.

Kai and Brian decided to check out the slapstick marathon that Becky had no desire to experience, ever. "That's why there's something for everyone," Kai said as she pushed him in the direction of the marathon and turned back to check on the venue for the finals of the World Poker Face Tournament. The barns and abandoned farmhouse at the distant end of the field added to the delicious bizarreness of the day.

Becky inhaled deeply as she walked by the food tents. The local restaurants had outdone themselves with the opportunity to showcase their wares, and there were patrons in every tent. But the air was filled with the sweet smokiness of slow-cooked Kansas City barbecue. Becky would definitely return later for some of that.

She heard the soundtracks coming from the voting booth for the most contagious laugh contest. The winner would get a free t-shirt with the festival logo and a version of their take-home message: *Joy is an inside-out issue.*

Becky loved the transparency of the day. They weren't seeding clouds or otherwise manipulating behavior without a person's consent. They had simply created welcoming conditions; inhibitions were being released by choice. As noted on the back of the program: *You decide when you want to laugh. Once the decision is made, the context hardly matters.*

She entered the makeshift arena surrounded by bleachers, which were mostly empty before the big event. The field, however, was covered with at least three hundred chairs, all filled with people facing each other, surrounded by spectators. They were there for the screening rounds of the World Poker Face Tournament, where random participants were paired off and instructed to stare until one of them cracked a smile. Anyone who could hold on for three minutes advanced to the semi-finals.

Becky climbed to the back of the bleachers and watched for a while. An elementary-aged boy and a white-haired man stared each other down for about four minutes until another kid made a remark that sent the adults into a fit of laughter. The boy and man both advanced to the next round, where Becky lost them in the crowd. A teenage girl was "randomly" paired with a boy about her age—the judges were volunteers, not the Olympic committee—but she only lasted about thirty seconds before she melted in a mess of giggles with her friends behind her. The boy turned red, but Becky was pleased to see the two groups of teenagers exiting together. Most of the pairings didn't last much more than a minute, young or old, male or female. It wasn't easy to stare into the eyes of a stranger while other strangers watched.

The event was Becky's favorite because it did the most to expand community connections, which formed the base of the contagion they were trying to spark. She wanted to believe that once people made eye contact with strangers in a positive environment, they would be more likely to make eye contact with strangers on the street. She thought that at least two people paired up at the festival would say hi to each other in the supermarket. It was a step in the right direction, beyond mere politeness toward I-see-you-and-I'm-glad-you-exist.

She stood up from the bleachers and stretched her legs. She found the logistics foreman, and he assured her that all glitches had been worked out and the screens were set up for the afternoon's big event where the final ten pairs would have a showdown in front of the crowd. A reporter had been around asking questions and taking pictures, he told her. She thanked him and said not to worry.

They hadn't invited any news media to cover the event, partly to avoid answering questions that might ruin the levity of the day. Their identities were far from secret, but there was no need to make themselves accessible. They agreed on a standard response to provide if pressed to make a statement:

the town needed a laugh, so it was money well spent. If necessary, they would explain how they came up with the idea over a backyard barbecue and make it all sound very innocuous. So far, the party line had been enough to prevent anyone from digging up old news about Dmitri and their disgraceful exit from New Tech.

Reassured that the logistics were in competent hands, Becky went back to the festival area to find Aiyana. She decided to check the laughter calisthenics and smile workout tents first. Aiyana was not there, but Becky said hello to the physical therapist and the professor in between their much-shortened sessions, and she gave them candied apples that she had picked up on her way back from the arena. She spotted Aiyana about a hundred yards away at the tent Kai and Brian had added at the last minute. She caught Aiyana's eye then waved and made her way through the crowd, nodding and smiling to at least a dozen strangers along the way.

Aiyana was standing beneath a sign displaying the title of the tent: "For People Who Were Dragged to This Event Against Their Will". She crossed her arms as Becky approached. "I don't recall approving this."

Becky grinned. "We made it for you."

Aiyana rolled her eyes but didn't restrain the muscles pulling at the corners of her mouth. Inside the tent were men and women watching sports on big screens, a couple of parents placating discomposed children, elderly gentlemen reading newspapers, and teenagers playing video games and texting, apparently amongst each other. One girl about thirteen years old was curled up on the ground reading a book. She wore overalls and a pink bandanna, and her face was as content as any Becky had seen that day.

By mid-afternoon, many groups with children had left, visibly tired, but with very little of the grouchiness visible at a zoo or amusement park at closing time. However, thousands more stayed until the four o'clock bell, when they grabbed their free dinners and drinks and headed to the bleachers for the big event. Becky found Brian and Kai rounding up their barbecue and root beer while Aiyana searched for sushi. They met up in their reserved section at the top of the bleachers.

The final ten poker face finalists were seated in a row of paired seats, the only ground spectacle. Their faces were shown on several split screens placed around the arena. The master of ceremonies explained the rules: neither contestant could show the merest twitch of the twelve smile muscles, or the round would be called in favor of the opponent. The top five remaining plus a sixth who lasted next longest would be paired off, then the top three plus a fourth, then down to the final two. The MC called the start of the event, and the contestants began to stare.

The audience watched the screens quietly for about fifteen seconds before a ripple of whispers began, growing louder as the minute wore one, until the MC said, "Is it just me, or is there something askew about watching people watch people?" A collective chuckle passed through the crowd, and the MC cued technicians to turn on the other half of the split screens. A sampling of videos from the day appeared: a random collection of ridiculous cats, dogs, and squirrels; a collage of participants, including grown men and women drenched and coasting down a slip 'n slide; and teenagers, retirees, and newfound friends erupting in silent laughter. The crowd responded whenever they saw people they knew or a video they remembered, and bursts of laughter bounced off the bleachers and into the twilight sky. The distracted contestants dropped off one by one and were re-paired until the final two were left: a man and woman, both in their early thirties.

The split screen went dark and showed the final two contestants and their first names, and a hush settled over the crowd, except for a few whistles and shouts of encouragement. The screen turned on again to pan the audience. The MC said the video was streaming live on the website, so each section cheered as the camera passed by, around the arena and back again. The MC said, "Just kidding, there is no live streaming, but that took up a good minute." Then a fully uniformed marching band burst onto the field. A couple of trombone players snuck up next to the two contestants and proceeded to play John Philip Sousa, stretching the slide terribly close but not quite touching the contestants' noses. Neither one flinched until both trombone players emptied their spit valves onto the ground between them. Both contestants broke eye contact and jumped back, knocking over their chairs.

The woman landed on the ground, grimacing. Giving in to his laughter, the man reached out a hand to help her to her feet. She smiled and shook her head then hopped up, wiping the back of her pants with her free hand. The Master of Ceremonies said, "Congratulations, you're both the grouchiest people in Freedom." He turned to the man. "Are you married?" The man shook his head. "No wonder." He turned to the woman. "Are you married?" She shook her head. The MC faced the audience and said, "There you go, a match made in heaven. Good night."

As the crowd filed down the bleacher aisles, Becky marveled at the orderliness of it all. There was an air of exhaustion but contentment, too. Or maybe she was projecting her own thoughts.

When she reached the field and started toward the exit, she felt a drop on her head. She tapped Aiyana on the shoulder and pointed up. Through a break in the clouds was a ball of light not seen in quite some time. Then it happened—millions of raindrops that had been holding their breath for months raced out of the sky to dance on every upturned face and outstretched hand in a homecoming parade reflected in the sun glinting off the bleachers. Hundreds by hundreds, they rolled into the thirsty grass and released the earth to the air.

54

Brian's text message arrived three days after the festival: *No change in data.*

Aiyana read it and felt a pang of disappointment. She knew an afternoon of smiling was not going to save the world, yet she let herself get caught up in the hope of it all. She reminded herself to manage her expectations in the future. Contentment is about temperance: A day of rain clears the air, but a week will drag you down. Fresh air is a balance of positive and negative ions. Neither energy nor prayer alone can fully heal. Don't be too pessimistic or too hopeful.

Across town, Becky read the message and felt elated. The danger was stalled. She knew that laughter alone couldn't wipe out insanity or evil, but she wholeheartedly believed it could give strength to average people who needed a little help, empowering them to reach out to others. Then when spring appeared, the white rabbit would show up against the backdrop.

Reason versus Heart
Idealism v. Realism
Fear vs. Hope

Fate versus random particles
An object in motion v. an object at rest
Equilibrium vs. equality

Infinity versus Death
Deist v. Atheist
North vs. South

Equal and Opposite
Balance of Neutrality
Fair yet Free

The epic battle rages inside,
 always against forever.

A week after the festival, Becky found a petition in her inbox at school. A note was handwritten at the top of the page: *Let's not live in fear of our kids. Let's not strip them of their potential.* The remaining message was a typed plea to dismantle the metal detector. She immediately signed her name and walked to the far corner of the building to return the page to its originator, an advanced placement history teacher in her first year at Freedom. Becky chided herself for being too caught up in her own concerns to properly welcome her new colleague.

The petition had only garnered a handful of signatures so far, but Becky was relieved to know that the kids had a few advocates at least. She knocked on the door to the history classroom. The new teacher was barely more than a teenager herself, stylishly dressed and with bright eyes and an aura that reached out at least two feet. Her classroom felt fresh and somehow safe. Becky had finally found a peer.

The teacher rose, and they met each other in the middle of the room. Becky handed over the paper and said, "Thank you for doing this."

The response was a shake of the head. "No, thank *you*. There are awful things in the world, and we have to be aware of them, but we don't have to feel them constantly, every minute of every day. I had forgotten that until the festival."

Becky felt tears welling up and a lump forming in her throat. So she simply nodded, and they shook hands, holding on in alliance.

While Becky drove home, a text message arrived from Brian: *% down by 5.*

57

Brian texted the team every few days with percentage changes showing the likelihood of catastrophe decreasing to 70% then 60%, until the end of May, when it was back below 50%. Becky invited everyone for a celebratory dinner. She told Brian to bring the graphs; she wanted to frame them.

The dinner was filled with exhilaration and possibility. Kai said the bi-monthly crime statistics had been released, and petty crime had fallen to its lowest rate all year. He had been thinking of a new risk management design, based on their success with the festival. The Smile Squad, as he called it, would be deployed to other epicenters, and Brian could publish the data as an intervention study—if indeed the results turned out the same.

They still conceded that the rain could have been the cause of their success, but the result no one could deny was the changing pattern. The wave phase has shifted so the overlap with nearby areas was minimal, meaning even if something were to happen in Freedom, it wouldn't be likely to spread. There was still uncertainty in the coming days, but in that uncertainty, there was hope.

Brian talked through the whole meal, as though he had years of words waiting to be used. Becky was happy to see it.

She went to the kitchen to prepare dessert and could still hear his animated voice telling Aiyana and Kai about the mass data modeling conference he had attended over the weekend. "I haven't been to a conference in years," he said. "It was fascinating! Also... I met someone. Her name is Lexi."

Becky froze, her knife full of frosting poised above the cake. She listened to Aiyana's overly chipper voice ask, "Who is this chick? What is she like?"

"She's not a chick," Brian said. "She's a scientist. She's super smart and gorgeous. Kind of like you, only nice."

Aiyana said, "I'll take that as a compliment. So is this serious or what?"

"No, we only had dinner. And some great conversations. But it's nice to get out again." Brian stopped talking, and she heard the scraping of a chair. Kai appeared in the doorway to the kitchen.

Becky forced her hand to lower the knife, to spread the frosting, back and forth, back and forth. Kai stood in the corner with his arms folded, not saying anything. Becky was glad for once that he tended to clam up in difficult situations.

Although her reaction surprised her, it's shouldn't have; of course she couldn't yank out feelings that had been rooted for a decade without expecting some residual weeds. Tears pricked at her eyes, which was silly. She wanted Brian to be happy, she did. Whatever fantasy there had once been, she had chosen not to act on it months ago. Her marriage was in a good place, so why was she upset? Because Brian had already found someone better than her? No, self-deprecating thoughts were a habit; she didn't believe them any more.

It was the finality that shocked her. There was nothing uncertain or unstated any more; he was moving on from their friendship, and so was she. That was a good thing, it was. She just needed a moment to mourn before letting go.

She swallowed hard a couple of times then looked over to Kai. "You know I love you, right?" she said. He winked, evoking a memory of their first meeting. A tear dropped onto the counter, and she knew it would be the last one she would ever shed over Brian.

Later, Brian showed them the new graphs, and he pointed out all the white noise signaling the random movement of energy—a positive change from the clumped, static patterns they had been seeing before. Becky's moment of sadness primed her to see, not a page full of light, but the dark spots among them all. She followed the darkness through the daily graphs, and her breath caught. She thought of Dmitri. And Dillon.

58

When Aiyana arrived home after the celebratory dinner, she put her leftover cake in the freezer then stood in the middle of her cold, empty kitchen. The stool where Brian had sat while he spewed his apocalyptic theories was pushed back neatly into its spot under the breakfast bar. He was the only one who had sat in it during the three years she had lived there.

She wanted to believe the worst was over, that the catastrophe had been averted. She had focused on the brightness in the data because she was tired of feeling frustrated, anxious, and conflicted. She wished she could as easily ignore the disharmony born within her. Across the hollow living room, the painting above the mantle glared back at her. That incongruous mix of cultures had shaped how people perceived her and how she had perceived the world since she was old enough to observe it. As much as she wanted to believe otherwise, she knew that some misperceptions couldn't be corrected by an afternoon of laughter.

Suddenly, she felt exhausted. She made her way to nearest chair and collapsed into it.

Maybe if she had grown up like Becky, exposed to a single set of beliefs and insulated from all others, life would be easier. But Aiyana had experienced too much. Her father was a staunch Baptist, but when the congregations began to dwindle at all the area churches, he considered it a crisis and proposed that the faith community find a way to integrate. His suggestion served to highlight the divides. The very thought of evangelicals joining forces with the reluctants—or heaven forbid, the Catholics—elicited gasps of blasphemy. So Aiyana had understood as early as elementary school that different denominations could have the same God but incompatible beliefs.

She might have been able to reconcile those conflicts in her mind, if she hadn't also grown up on the reservation where there were many like her mother who had converted to Christianity—or been converted, as Aiyana viewed it—but still held on to their traditional beliefs. Traditions varied among nations, and her mother tried to explain the basic principles in terms of parallels, equating the supreme deities Kisiihiat and Mi-chi Ogaw-maw to the one true God, suggesting the hero Wisaaka was like Jesus, and demoting *manitooaki* spirit messengers and other deities to angel equivalents. Others vehemently disagreed with her mother's approach, until eventually, Aiyana decided that all religion was mythology.

Her decision had solidified after her grandmother died, and her mother took Aiyana to China to meet her grandfather. The sights and sounds of the country had overwhelmed most of her memories of the trip, but she clearly recalled two things about the man who'd had the mysterious short-lived romance with her grandmother. The first was that he moved like a twenty-year-old, although he was a ninety if he was a day. The second was that every afternoon, he folded himself into a meditation pose and could not be disturbed.

Aiyana liked the idea of quieting her mind, which was always racing with thoughts, so she had joined him on several occasions, although she made no effort to learn about his beliefs. She didn't care whether he was Buddhist or Taoist or Christian or Muslim or anything else. She had had enough of religion. Besides, such personal questions were hardly appropriate to pose to a virtual stranger.

She had risen at dawn on most days so she could explore the area for a couple of hours on her own. One morning, after her conspicuous height and too-dark skin received more than the usual number of wary scowls from villagers, she ventured into a Buddhist temple where she thought she might be welcome. While she was there, she was surprised to learn that Buddha was not a god at all, but merely a person who strived for enlightenment and desired to end suffering through elimination of ignorance. Her sixteen-year-old mind latched onto the simplicity of the idea.

Over the years, she had defined her beliefs further in the context of her own experiences and away from the Buddhist tradition. But her present mind recalled something else she had heard back then—that the root of all suffering is the subtle dissatisfaction with life's constant changes. What was it Becky had said? Uncertainty can be the cornerstone of hope or the foundation of fear. Aiyana supposed it depended on the architect.

Her teenage self had also warmed to the idea of a system of causality running through the universe, but not created by a god. She had been a little uncomfortable with giving up the concept of having a permanent soul, but based on the many different customs surrounding religion, and every person believing in theirs as strongly as everyone else, the only logical conclusion in her mind was that God and Kisiihiat and Mi-chi Ogaw-maw do not exist.

She had refused to go to any church thereafter. Her father didn't push her except for the weekend of high school graduation, when he wanted to send her off with prayers and a laying-on of hands. She grew angry at him for not respecting her beliefs. "Don't I always try to do the right thing? Am I not planning to make good with my life? What more do you want from me?" she asked. "My Aiyana," he said, "you're trying to perpetrate good on people. You think of them as a helpless herd of animals, beneath you, and indistinguishable. But the best shepherdess knows each of her flock by name."

While she contemplated the picture on the mantle in her stark surroundings in Freedom, Kansas, she remembered something Brian had once said: Religion is a man-made thing, not the same as God. A car passed on the street outside, and the headlights shone through the curtain, bending over the furniture and up and across the wall.

A thought struck her about the duality of light. If measured one way, it looks like a wave, but measured another way, it looks like a particle. Two different observers could see two different things. So, was the logical conclusion that light doesn't exist, that it's only a myth?

She jumped up from the chair and shook the thought out of her head. They were all ganging up on her—Brian, Becky, her parents. Practical doubt was hard to maintain in the center of so much certainty. She attempted the elliptical machine for a few minutes, but she was too tired to bother. She decided to take a shower and call it a day, hoping her mind would feel clearer in the morning.

The steam rose around her as the hot water poured over her head and cascaded down her face and shoulders. Why was it still so hard for her to find contentment? The team had succeeded, and the others were blissfully moving ahead; why couldn't she? Brian's announcement about meeting someone had caught her off guard, and Aiyana had to admit that she felt jealous. She didn't begrudge him a little happiness after all he had put himself through, but at least while he had been holed up in his lab focusing on his research, she hadn't felt alone in her devotion to her work. She began to wonder whether it was devotion or intentional distance that sent her home alone every night.

She liked to spend time by herself, which had always been true. Yet she had never been a recluse like Brian; she interacted with people daily. Of course, it was also true that Becky was the only person in Freedom whom Aiyana might call a friend. Becky was the only one who knew how much she was at odds with the worlds she functioned in: an atheist living on the edge of the Bible Belt and an alternative healer in the medical establishment. But Becky didn't know Aiyana's biggest secret—that she was Dmitri's Judas.

Ironically, Kai could probably understand her better than Becky could, having jealousy and secrets of his own. She suspected he didn't have much in the way of faith, either. She turned off the shower and grabbed her fluffiest towel. Maybe that's why he and Becky fit. Becky had enough faith for the both of them, but she needed someone to steer through the real world. Alone, they each would drown, but together, they kept afloat. Such co-existence might be nice, Aiyana thought.

She watched herself in the mirror while she brushed her teeth. Rosiness from the heat of the shower infused her dark cheeks. She stared into her own eyes, holding herself accountable for her thoughts.

Her patients had been asking her to re-start their energy therapy. She told them that they already had the power within themselves and didn't need her therapy. But she had begun to wonder whether she had lied. Alone, their desire to heal wasn't strong enough to restore balance; and alone, her energy therapy couldn't force a change; but together, the synergy might be enough to cure disease. Maybe two observers couldn't understand fully until they put their observations together.

Her head was so tired. Too much thinking. She crawled into bed and curled under the blankets and tried to quiet her mind. She drifted to sleep, repeating a comforting mantra: *I am a good shepherdess. I know all of my patients by name, and I don't think they're helpless at all.*

59

Becky felt like a different person the day after Brian's revelation. She allowed herself to think about it while she reviewed her lesson plan before class. A part of their closeness was gone, that constant warmth like a pet's weight at the foot of the bed, something she could touch whenever she wanted to feel comfort. In its place was a void but also a strange lightness akin to freedom. She had lost something familiar, but it had never been part of her foundation.

The more she thought about it, the less she considered it a loss. The cobwebs of Brian had been obscuring a statue of Kai, neglected but still solid, more like a cornerstone than anything she had ever known aside from her faith. She had agreed to his marriage proposal as a shallow child, hardly imagining that something deeper was waiting to be found. Had he been aware of it? Or was the real fairy tale of their relationship the part where Prince Charming and the princess fall in love without even knowing each other?

While the students straggled in, Becky wrapped up her thoughts with the realization that she and Kai had been faking their marriage like a forced Duchenne smile. Finally, their brains were kicking in and making it real.

Dillon took his place in the back row and put his head down on the desk. His hair was clean and neatly combed, and in his oversized sweatshirt and baggy jeans, he had no resemblance to Dmitri. Yet, adrenaline raced through Becky's veins as she remembered the pattern she had seen in Brian's data and the unwanted recognition of it.

Thought she had seen. The pattern might not have been the same.

Still, it raised questions. How could she believe their team could change a whole community but not believe she could help this one child? Had she been hiding in her prayers, protecting herself with an excuse of God's will, and sitting back waiting for a miracle to touch the boy, while she was right there within heart's reach? Maybe Becky herself was supposed to be his miracle, and all the time, she had just been watching him suffer. She had let Dmitri down, but she wouldn't allow it to happen again, data or no data.

With the bell about to ring, she hastily scribbled a note on her pad then ripped the page off and walked nonchalantly toward the back of the room to slide it under Dillon's elbow. He barely lifted his head when he read it: *You are not invisible.* His eyes behind the arm of his sweatshirt scanned the class until he saw her standing at the door. The bell rang, and he put his head back down.

Becky wasn't so naïve as to think that a note or a smile or a laugh could change the heart of an angry criminal or someone determined to do harm. But any one of those things could help a person on the verge feel not quite as desperate. Dillon was no more angry at heart than Dmitri had been. She was convinced of that, convinced he simply felt trapped inside something and couldn't find a way out. By letting him know she could see him, she was providing him an exit. Eyes are windows.

The next day she slipped him another note: *You're not stuck.*

The next day: *I can help you handle it.*

The third time, he looked up and, ever so briefly, met her eyes.

60

Aiyana leaned on the doorjamb, one foot in Dmitri's room and one still in the corridor. She had asked Brian to bring her on his visit, much to his surprise, but her courage had been failing her all morning.

She took stock of the bare surroundings where Dmitri had spent the past nine years: one bed, one lamp, one table. Nothing that would be a danger to himself or others. The room was blank, as though he had withdrawn his presence from the world, and with it, dragged the color from the walls, the curtains, and the carpeting, leaving only a bed, a lamp, a table. Even his t-shirt was blank.

She had always told herself that Dmitri was either brain dead or insane, and by being labeled a criminal, he at least had medical care and a place to live. Becky and Brian wanted to believe his mind was intact and he was choosing not to speak, waging a prolonged rebellion against authority. Aiyana had to find out which theory was right before she could release her secret guilt.

Seeing Dmitri's red head, dull and flecked with gray, bowed over the graphs Brian had brought, Aiyana knew why she had never come before and never intended to. It was too sad to see a once great mind now fried and silent. Brian told him all they had been doing since his last visit, about the festival and the theories and the data, but Aiyana knew it was pointless.

Yet she believed—had to believe—that it was just. She thought of Dennis Greeley and his wedding and his family. Dmitri was paying for part of his crimes, too. Dmitri had probably been beyond saving, so at least one of them had been redeemed. He truly did belong in an institution. One bed, one lamp, one table.

Aiyana realized that she had never seen where Dmitri lived before. She didn't know whether his room had been cluttered with dusty textbooks and dirty socks or orderly like physics and sparse like the orphanage. She didn't know where he would go if given the choice, or how he would live. She wanted to believe that he was in the best place for him, but how did she know? And would he agree?

A sheaf of papers cascaded to the floor. Brian bent to pick them up, mumbling an apology. Dmitri's eyes were boring into Aiyana's forehead, and she shivered. Yes, Dmitri needed to be there. She had done the best she could in a bad situation.

She helped Brian gather the graphs, pulling one from Dmitri's table while his finger still dragged upon it. She hugged the pages to her chest and left the room, Dmitri's eyes on her all the while. Brian followed her as she walked quickly down the hallway, anxious to leave her mistake behind. Until her mind registered something she had seen—the dark spots in the trail of Dmitri's finger. A pattern that was seared into her brain.

Surely Brian would have mentioned anything of note; he'd been studying the data for weeks. But he wasn't searching for an individual predator. He could have forgotten what it looked like. He could have chosen to forget.

When they reached the car, Aiyana turned around and raced back to the room. Dmitri was sitting where they had left him, still staring at the door, as though waiting for her to return. "It's the same, isn't it?" she asked, needing his confirmation for the strength to do the right thing, to reveal her secret. Dmitri's green irises darted like lightning. She had to ask the question, but she refused to get on her knees to do it. If he didn't answer, she would walk away. Finally, Dmitri nodded. It was slight. If she had blinked, she would have missed it.

Aiyana was sure of what she saw, and it terrified her. He was physically locked up, but he was free in his mind. Aiyana shuddered at the thought of his imprisonment, and her skin crawled with the guilt that was hers and hers alone. Whatever she had thought he deserved, the debt was paid. He was still alive and dying in captivity, and she was the one with the key to his cage.

She didn't let herself think to the next step and its implication on her career. First, she had to tell Brian about Dennis Greeley and make him see that Becky was still in danger.

I can't leave, but I must leave, avoid danger.
Avoid it or face it, it doesn't matter. Fear controls you.
Acknowledge it, embrace it, use it, ride it.
Fear is energy. A kinetic coil. Potential. Possessed.
Let Go.
Addiction, adrenaline, surge.

"We've been thinking of violence in terms of waves," Aiyana said, "but a perpetrator is a particle." The pages she was holding against the hood of the car flapped in the wind, threatening to blow away before she could make Brian listen.

He said, "You can't apply quantum principles to a macro environment. Psychology isn't—"

"Brian," she interrupted. "I'm trying to show you—"

"I can't see," he said, standing back. "We need more data..."

"We have enough. You have had enough for a long time." She reached a hand around his back and pulled him gently toward the car—one step, then another. "There have been two things going on at the same time: the conditions for random violence, and a specific, pre-meditated act. The tension that created the first was masking the second."

His hands began to shake.

"But we cleared the cloud away." She tried to reassure him. "We did the right thing." She took a deep breath. "The pattern is peaking, like before, and there's something else you need to know." She told him everything about Dennis Greeley and what she saw and did. Brian stood face-to-face with her, not blinking while she talked. When she stopped, he didn't move, although she could almost hear the gears in his brain rewinding the past nine years and revising his assumptions in light of the new data. His face was inscrutable; he could have been angry, or he could have been relieved. She hadn't thought before about how her secret might have influenced his life, too. She didn't want to think about it.

He reached for her wrist and lifted her hand from the hood. The graphs blew across the parking lot, and she made a move to chase them. "Let it go," he said. Then he got into the driver's seat, and they returned Freedom, not speaking one word to each other the whole way.

63

If I were Brian, I would have pushed Aiyana out of the car as soon as we hit the highway. But I've never been Brian, and he didn't ask me. In fact, I didn't even know that my wife was still in danger because all the way from New Tech to Freedom, neither Brian nor Aiyana thought to call me. I was invisible to them like always, forgotten in my own damn story, and I resent it still. I should have been there.

My anger has had room to fester, but Brian's didn't. As he told me later, during those two hours with Aiyana in the car, he couldn't bring himself to hate her.

At first he imagined how different his life would have been, how much of his self had been worn away by the ever-present guilt. His anger spun around his own perspective, rising until a movement of Aiyana's hand brought him back to the complex reality. Whether or not Dmitri had been the bomber didn't change the fact that he had lost his mind, which didn't change the fact that Brian felt responsible for driving him to the edge. His anger deflated like a burned-out tire.

Then he began to think about the influence her secret had had on his research. Our entire enterprise had been shaped by the missing piece of data. Brian had put all of his efforts into measuring aggregate energy, carefully ensuring that no one knew the measurements were occurring, convinced that negative attention alone had created Dmitri's outcome, in the absence of any real threat. Had he known the truth was a combination of perception and reality—that the energy patterns had indeed tracked a perpetrator, one whose actions were independent of our observations—his research might have been more balanced, more applicable. He might have published his findings. We might have acted sooner. We might have saved lives.

Aiyana had taken control, decided what was best for everyone, not bothering to consider all the consequences. As much as she despised Dmitri, she resembled him in her arrogance. I don't believe she deserved to be forgiven.

Brian's anger couldn't stretch so far. In his mind, Aiyana was heartless and calculating and cold, but in the seat next to him, she was warm, and she was worried. He couldn't help imagining her as a student, scared like the rest of us, not knowing what to do, and wishing none of it had happened. Like the rest of us, she hadn't been able to leave it behind. Her own energy practice was rooted in our project, and she wrote a yearly confession in her cards to Dennis Greeley. Her friendship with Becky may even have started as a kind of penance, too.

Brian wouldn't have dared to focus attention on a suspect the way Aiyana had, but he couldn't begrudge the results. Because by keeping her secret, and reminding Dennis Greeley that she expected him to live right, he somehow had managed to do so.

By the time they crossed the town line into Freedom, Brian had forgiven Aiyana and developed a working theory: Negative expectations increase the chance for negative outcomes and likewise for positive, not only because of the light in which we choose to view the outcome but also because the choice of light is a catalyst for the action. Had he bothered to call me then, I would have asked him what theory could explain why suddenly Dennis Greeley was back at the center of the looming violence.

64

It was a little after one o'clock when Brian and Aiyana pulled up to Freedom High School. Becky hadn't answered her phone, but she rarely did during school hours. Aiyana rushed into the office and asked for the guidance counselor. She said it was an urgent matter. "On the last day of school?" the receptionist asked. The precipitous timing clicked in Aiyana's brain. She felt Brian tense beside her.

When Dennis Greeley emerged from his office, he stopped at the sight of them. "Where is Becky?" Aiyana asked. He shook his head, seeming perplexed as he ushered them into his office and closed the door. He paged Becky while Aiyana and Brian launched ahead with their accusations, trying to describe the research without data to show him. He insisted that he had no intention of hurting anyone.

Frustrated, Aiyana confused the matter further by telling him that he needed to come forward about Dmitri because it was the right thing to do. She said Dmitri was locked up in a mental ward for a crime he didn't commit, and she and Dennis were to blame. Volunteering in the facility could never right such a wrong.

Dennis's face went pale. "But my wife…our kids…"

Aiyana had plenty to lose herself. She never should have trusted him. She and Brian stepped forward and towered over his desk. For a minute, she thought he might call for help, but of course, he wouldn't risk exposing the secrets. How had her life become such a mess? And where was Becky?

That's when they heard the gunshot.

The earth stood still, every electron frozen in orbit. Their first thought was: release. The event had been a long time coming. The second thought: confusion. If not Dennis, then who? Third: location. Where was Becky's classroom and which direction did the shot come from? They heard a car alarm. *Beep. Beep. Beep. Beep.* Then they were up, moving toward the parking lot. A surge of administrators and staff held back the curious students. The principal was on his cell phone while he yelled at Dennis and Aiyana and Brian to come back. Instead, they broke into a run.

They ran toward the car horn until they could see an open trunk. They slowed to approach. Behind the trunk was a boy, pressing himself back against the bumper of a truck, its alarm triggered by the same shock that had formed a spider web crack in the driver's side windshield. The boy's face stood out like paper against his plaid shirt, and he was looking down. Their eyes followed his gaze to Becky, lying on the ground in a pool of blood.

Time returned full speed. Dennis Greeley dialed 9-1-1 and called for an ambulance. Brian and Aiyana dropped to the ground. Brian touched Becky's face. "Becky!" he said. "Can you hear me?" Aiyana scanned for the wound. The upper left sleeve of the blue school t-shirt was dark with blood. Aiyana got up and leaned over the trunk to search for a first aid kit.

"Be careful!" the boy shouted, his voice thin but clear. That's when she saw the duffel bag and the dark hole, still smoking.

She gingerly lifted the first aid kit from the opposite side of the trunk. She ransacked the box for several packages of gauze and ripped them open. She gently peeled up Becky's shirtsleeve and lifted her arm to check for an exit wound. There it was. Becky's eyelids fluttered. She was conscious but barely. Aiyana pressed a stack of gauze to each side of the wound and sat on the ground, cradling the injured arm in her lap.

Brian was on the other side, his left hand under Becky's head, stroking her hair with his right. He leaned down to her ear. "It's going to be okay," he kept saying over and over, to the rhythm of the car horn. They stared at Becky's ashen face, and they waited.

Beep. Beep. Beep. Beep.

Years passed before they heard the sound of sirens. Dennis Greeley snapped to attention and grabbed the boy by the shoulders. "Dillon, what happened?" The boy was still staring at Becky.

"It was an accident," he said.

"But what happened?" Dennis asked again.

The sirens came closer, and Becky stirred. Her eyelids fluttered open again, and she tried to focus on Brian then Aiyana. "Tell them it was an accident," she murmured.

The emergency vehicles screamed into the parking lot, followed by the police. Brian and Aiyana told Becky one last time that it was going to be okay while the paramedics moved in to do their job.

As she stood aside and watched them work, Aiyana didn't feel anger, just numbness. Brian stood next to her, where the police had placed him while they carefully removed the duffel bag from the trunk. Brian put an arm around Aiyana, and she felt it there, was glad for it, but didn't move.

"Did you all see what happened?" the policeman asked.

The three adults shook their heads. Dillon said quietly, "Yes." Dennis put his hand on the boy's arm as if to stop him.

The policeman watched the movement, and his focus slid up to Dennis Greeley's face. "Whose car is this?" he asked.

Dennis said, "It's mine."

Beep. Beep. Beep. Beep. Beep.

The paramedics lifted Becky onto a stretcher and wheeled her into the ambulance, and with sirens blaring, they drove away. A second police officer walked across the lot, followed by a student who unlocked the truck, all the while staring—not at the blood on the ground, or the bullet hole in the windshield, but at Dennis and Dillon. *Get a good look,* Aiyana wanted to say. *Make sure you get the details right when you report this to your friends.*

The horn finally stopped. The silence that followed hurt Aiyana's ears.

The policeman told the truck's owner to go back to the school lobby; they'd let him know when he could take the vehicle home. The student lumbered off. Dillon and Dennis stared a hole in his back as he went.

"The folks down there say they don't know anything," the police officer told his partner, who was still eyeing Dennis.

"This young man was about to tell us what happened." The officer gestured to Dillon.

Dennis said, "We'd like to talk with a lawyer."

Dillon snatched his arm away. "It was an accident, Dad. Why can't I just tell the truth?"

"You can. We all will." He looked over at Aiyana.

The policeman noticed. He turned his attention to Brian and Aiyana. Brian's arm was still around her. "And you two are...?"

His voice was full of suspicion. Aiyana couldn't blame him. They were all acting as though they had reasons to fear the police. Of course, they did. It was too complicated to explain, standing there in the parking lot next to Becky's lifeblood soaking the pavement in front of them. "We're friends," Brian said.

Then Dillon started to talk. "I tried to tell you." His father protested, but the boy spoke into the pool of blood as if it were a confessional drawing him in. "I knew things would change when my sister got pregnant. I hated him. Everyone does." He lashed out a leg toward the now-silent truck, and Aiyana realized the boyfriend was the student they had seen a minute before. One of the policemen turned his head toward the school, but he stayed put. "I knew as soon as people found out, she wouldn't be popular any more. I warned her, but she never understood how bad it could be." He looked up at Dennis.

"You guys said, 'She's a teenager; she'll do what she wants.' Well, she wanted someone to care."

Brian, Aiyana, and Dennis listened without moving. They had all been clinging to their secrets for so long that it was strangely liberating to watch the boy release his truth, regardless of what would follow.

Dillon's eyes fell back to the stain on the pavement. "Just because we're teenagers, people treat us like delinquents, and no matter what we do, it proves what they already decided. A lot of teachers think that way, too, but Mrs. Inoue never did."

Aiyana didn't like his use of the past tense, and she felt Brian's grip tighten around her shoulder.

"She wasn't supposed to get hurt."

One of the policemen cleared his throat and said, "No one is under arrest at the moment, but let's all go down to the station where you can tell us your story from the beginning."

Aiyana somehow always knew it would come back to this. Except now, she and Dennis would also tell the truth, consequences be damned.

Hours later, Brian and Aiyana arrived at the hospital. Kai met them inside the emergency room door. "She's in recovery," he said. "She's going to be okay. The bone in her upper arm was shattered, but they said with physical rehab, she should be fine. What—?" Dennis and Dillon came in behind them, and Kai looked stunned.

Aiyana was confused. Brian hadn't had time to tell Kai much of anything about what had happened or who was involved. Then she realized that Kai wasn't looking at Dillon;

he was staring at Dennis. He probably recognized him from Becky's school, but a concerned colleague shouldn't induce shock. Unless it had something to do with the baby...

Dillon mumbled, "I'm sorry." Kai blinked. He turned to Brian, who led him away to explain.

65

Brian told me that while I was at the hospital praying for my wife to come through surgery, the kid Dillon and his stepfather Dennis and even Aiyana had spilled their guts to the police. Apparently, the kid and his sister used to be close, but when she got pregnant, they both bore the ridicule. He blamed the boyfriend. He and his friends talked about ways to make the guy hurt. Then they talked about hurting all of the people at school who had wronged them: the bullies who gave swirlies in the boys' toilet, the adults who let it happen, the cheaters who managed to deflect the blame, and the mean girls who made up lies online to torment the target of the week. They talked about avenging themselves and protecting the others. They talked about tricking and stabbing and shooting and bombing. Dillon joined in because he thought it was just talk, at first.

He wasn't sure when the imaginings turned real, but in any case, he didn't know what to do. He couldn't think of any person he could tell, teenager or adult, who would be less scared than he was. That was the first admission that struck a chord in me because such despair represented a massive failure of the adults in his life, Becky among them. Dillon figured if his friends wanted to shoot people, they were going to do it, and he couldn't stop them any more than his parents could stop his sister. So he tried to pretend he didn't know about it, but they kept pulling him in. He was afraid to tell, afraid not to tell, afraid to do something, afraid to do nothing.

It was at the hospital that I first learned from Brian what Aiyana and Dennis Greeley had been hiding all those years, which raised a lot of what-ifs when I later read a redacted part of the police transcript.

(Minor): Then they actually got guns. I tried to tell you.

Greeley: When?

(Minor): I asked you if I should call the police if I heard someone talking about guns. You said it might be just talk, that some people think about doing things they would never really do.

(Pause.)

Greeley: Why didn't you tell anyone else?

(Minor): Because they're all scared. The teachers don't stand up to the bullies, either. They know someone might swear at them or shoot them or beat up another kid if they try to interfere. Nobody knows what do. We're all stuck in this fishbowl, waiting for something bad to happen. Every day, I could feel it coming closer, and I wished I could disappear.

That was when my Becky started passing him the notes. It had scared him at first. He wondered how much she knew. Then he realized he wanted her to know.

(Minor): She expected us to respect each other, and she acted like all our opinions counted, no matter what happened outside of class. She was nice, but everyone knew she was in charge. I felt safe in her room. That's why I dared to ask if she ever got so far into something

that she couldn't get out. She said there's always a way out, but
sometimes you need help to see it.

He hadn't told about the situation then because he thought
he could go to jail for being so involved with the planning. But
Becky's comment started him thinking that maybe he could do
something.

The plan had been to hide the guns outside the building on
the last day of school. At the end of the day, they would fire at
the bus lines and through the windows to the halls and
everyone within reach; no one was exempt from the anger.
Dillon suggested that they transport the guns in the trunk of
his sister's car because he thought he could get her to come
outside at some point and drive away—for a personal
emergency, an urgent errand, anything to pass a couple of
hours until school would be over for the year and it wouldn't
matter any more.

But his sister had been in the nurse's office all morning.
Apparently, it wasn't unusual for her to go there when the
taunting became too much. I could certainly relate. I spent a lot
of time in the nurse's office myself with a fake allergy that
flared up whenever I didn't understand a concept I was
supposed to have already mastered.

Dillon waited for his sister until nearly noon, when he
asked for the keys, intending to drive the guns away by
himself. He reconsidered because he could be arrested for
driving without a license. That was the second admission that
struck a chord in me. Becky had told me a thousand times how
teenagers are still kids, but I didn't quite believe it until then. A
rational adult mind would know that preventing mass murder

would take priority over driving without a license, but to a teenager, the privilege of driving is the bigger, everyday reality. Dillon's thought process wasn't irrational; it was the perspective of a child.

So, as a last resort, he had found Becky and confessed. They had gone to the parking lot to move the guns to her car where they would be safe until she called the police.

Brian and I wondered why she tried to take care of it herself. Brian thought Becky had the same lingering fear that the rest of us had shared for nine years. Since Dillon had held onto the keys, he could easily have changed his mind and given his friends the guns if she had called the police, hastening the crisis.

I prefer to think she gave Dillon the benefit of the doubt. He was panicked, and she was trying to keep him calm and out of trouble, like she did for all her kids. She wanted to remove the immediate danger then call the police and tell them Dillon was a hero. Except she never got the chance.

I suppose it's possible that she was being entirely selfish, trying to prove she was strong, or clinging to the power of being a guardian over her kids. We were curious about all her reasons, but we never asked. In the end, the whys didn't matter.

The confessions hadn't stopped with Dillon. Brian had called me to check on Becky while Aiyana called my lawyer. She knew him from our work on the festival, and he referred her to a criminal attorney. Aiyana finally told everything she knew about Dmitri and the bomb and tracking Dennis. Dennis corroborated her story without protest, convinced that if he hadn't been keeping the secret, he would have reacted differently to what Dillon had asked him, and prevented the whole situation.

The lawyer told them that they could no longer be charged for obstruction of justice, but domestic terrorism had no statute of limitations. However, because neither Aiyana nor Dennis had actually set off a bomb, the district attorney wasn't expected to pursue the issue. Brian said the lawyer did warn them that the state might try to recoup Dmitri's medical costs, and he would consult his colleagues about how to handle it, but both Dennis and Aiyana readily agreed to pay any such price.

The paperwork and proceedings would take a while, but eventually, Dmitri would be free to leave the hospital if he chose to. The lawyer asked them where Dmitri would go if he couldn't afford to stay. Of course, Aiyana had never thought about it.

I had seen Dennis Greeley but hadn't met him before our encounter at the hospital, and I didn't know all those things about him. What I did know was that his daughter was a pregnant teenager registered with the adoption agency handling our case. I was the only one who knew.

So, when Brian and I returned to the antiseptic waiting room where Aiyana and Dillon and Dennis were standing awkwardly in the corner, waiting for word on Becky, I couldn't help listening when a phone rang. My mind started racing at what I thought I heard, and when Dennis confirmed to Dillon that the girl had gone into labor, I couldn't stop myself from saying, "Not now!"

66

Aiyana felt practically in cahoots with the legal establishment after two more visits to the Freedom police station, several meetings with her lawyer, and a trip to Cloud County where Dmitri's commitment had been handled. Everyone involved in the case wanted to clear Dmitri's name as soon as possible and move on. If they were lucky, the media would gloss over the case as well.

She stopped at the hospital gift shop on her way to Becky's room and ran into Brian, whom she had successfully been avoiding for the past several days since her big confession. "Oh, hey," he said when he saw her. She lifted her hand in a half-hearted hello. He held up a book. "Becky needed some reading material to take home with her." Aiyana nodded.

They stood, neither speaking, each engrossed in the closest dangling trinket, until they both breathed in and sighed heavily. Aiyana heard Brian chuckle.

"Listen," she said. "I'm sorry I..." She had been trying to think of what to say for days.

"Have you seen the news?" he said. "The most sensational headline was, 'Accidental shooting of teacher', and it wasn't even the top story. The police have handled the legalities quietly with all the minors involved, and since no one is pressing charges, the news story was a pretty sparse account. Especially since the only witness who's talking is the boyfriend, and being there for less than ten seconds, he has a reputation that precedes him. So, he's been marginalized." Aiyana met his eyes. "There's no way this is going to spread," he said.

She shook her head. "And no one is ever going to know how much worse it could have been. What we prevented."

"I'm okay with that," he said. "For now."

She finally smiled. "I think I am, too."

Then he reached over and hugged her.

Awkward.

He let go and laughed. "You're just as cuddly as ever."

She shrugged.

He handed her the book. "Why don't you take this up to Becky? I've got to crunch some numbers or something."

"What are you working on?" she asked.

"I don't know," he said, "and I mean that in the best way."

When Aiyana got to Becky's room, she knocked on the door, and Kai got up from his chair beside the bed. He kissed Becky on the forehead. "I'm going to get an ETA on those discharge papers." As he passed Aiyana, he told her, "Don't leave before I come back."

Aiyana said as she entered the room, "Wow, you're conscious. That's already better than the last two times I saw you."

Becky smiled. "Hey, stranger, nice of you to stop by."

"Yeah, sorry, I had a few things to do."

"I heard."

Aiyana read the cover of the book in her hand to avoid reading Becky's expression. The front flap was plastered with a *Bestseller!* label, but a price sticker obscured the blurb on the back. She held up the book. "I ran into Brian. He said you wanted this."

Becky was still watching her intently.

"I apologize," Aiyana said. "I shouldn't have kept such a secret from you all. Can you forgive me?" It didn't sound adequate, but she hoped Becky knew it was sincere.

Becky shook her head, and Aiyana couldn't breathe.

"It's not mine to forgive."

Aiyana didn't know how to answer. She felt at the same time relieved and more burdened than before.

"Have you talked to Dmitri?" Becky asked.

Aiyana backed up and leaned against a wall. "Not since…"

Becky didn't say anything.

Aiyana tried to fill the void. "It turns out a nun from the orphanage—I mean, children's home—has been visiting him regularly and even tried to get him released a couple of times over the years. My lawyer talked to her, and it turns out that she's been keeping a place for him to live. So she'll take him, if he wants to go."

"I didn't know any of that," Becky said.

"Yeah, well…"

Several moments of awkward silence passed.

"You have to talk to him," Becky said.

"I know, I just…"Aiyana collapsed into a chair. "He still hasn't spoken. Maybe he never will. Maybe he doesn't know anything that's going on around him, and I was only imagining…"

Becky reached over and laid her hand on the edge of the bed. Aiyana felt the gesture and appreciated it more than she would say. She nodded toward Becky's other arm, which was enclosed in a cast from her shoulder to her hand. "Does it hurt a lot?"

"To be honest, I don't feel much." She raised her eyebrows to the IV bag hanging next to the bed.

Aiyana's hand flew to her heart in exaggerated shock. "Becky Inoue! Are you using painkillers? An invasive, mood-altering, *drug*?"

Becky smirked. "I've gotten a little less…rigid since we've been friends. Not in the important things, mind you."

"Of course." Aiyana smiled. "Seriously, though, I'm glad you're okay."

"Aiyana Rivers! Is that a tear in your eye?"

Aiyana blinked it away. "Apparently, I've gotten soft hanging out with you, too."

A nurse came in to check Becky's vital signs. "Last time!" she said.

Becky asked her, "How's the baby?"

"Sweet as ever. You should go by the nursery on your way home and see her."

Aiyana didn't know how much to read into the exchange, so when the nurse left, she didn't bring it up. But Becky said, "Kai told me everything."

"She's the one, then?"

"We don't know; we haven't heard anything from the adoption agency. Now that everyone's sharing their secrets, Dennis and his family decided to keep the baby. The girl didn't want to give her up in the first place. So, if she was the one, she isn't any more." Becky sighed deeply. "Life is messy."

Aiyana couldn't argue with that.

"So," Becky said slowly, "have you given any further thought to what Kai and I asked you? About being our baby's godmother? Whenever we get her—or him?"

Aiyana stood up and began to pace. She hadn't figured out how to have this conversation, either. "The thing is...I think you and I work because we're polar. Magnetic opposites. We push and pull against each other, and even when our positions don't change much, the tension between us provides clarity like a compass. Do you know what I mean?" She wasn't at all sure her analogy made sense.

Becky said, "True North."

"Okay, yes...I think every person needs to find her own True North. What I'm trying to say is..." She leaned forward on the railing at the end of the bed, demanding Becky's focus. She had to say it but would only say it once. "I can't do it."

Becky nodded. "I know."

Aiyana wasn't surprised that Becky accepted her refusal without argument; a mother shouldn't want a reluctant guardian for her child. Still, it felt like a letdown. "Where does that leave us?"

"In the middle of a dialogue. Because that's what we do—we shake up the stagnation and shift the certainty. Energy happens in the movement. God is there in the act of connection."

Kai came in then with a doctor, followed by Brian with a wheelchair. Aiyana turned to them and pleaded, "Would you take her home already? Her nonsense is getting on my nerves."

Epilogue

Here is where I choose to end our story. My marriage to Becky was on the verge of a family; Brian's future was poised in the freedom of the unknown; and Aiyana was absolved, with Dmitri neither alive nor dead in his box of silence. Promise and disappointment co-existed in our future, neither one certain, and in that, was hope.

But you are the observer now, so the decision is yours. Will you forgive our transgressions and leave us here with the gift of all possibilities? Or will you choose to look further, to determine our fate, and what will you choose to see?

Aiyana's Eyes

Aiyana caught up with Becky and Kai walking hand-in-hand from the parking lot. "Did you see the rainbow?" Aiyana looked where Becky was pointing and glimpsed a faintly colored halo above the Home for Children.

Brian met them at the door, having come straight from his interview for a data consulting job in Washington, DC. A nun led them to Dmitri's room. It was barely better furnished than the mental hospital, but it felt homey, more so than Aiyana's own place did.

The nun told them that Dmitri hadn't spoken yet, but she was still optimistic. She knocked on the door, and he opened it. His red hair was clean and combed, and he was wearing a brand new, freshly pressed, purple cape. It seemed right on him.

Aiyana figured they might as well get the party started, so she handed him the gift bag she had brought. Dmitri pulled the t-shirt out of the bag with some difficulty due to a poorly healed arm from nine years prior, one of the many things left broken and untended in the immediacy of the aftermath. The nun helped him hold up the t-shirt: *Better to stay silent and be assumed a genius than to open your mouth and annoy someone.* Becky gasped. "That's so inappropriate," she whispered. Aiyana watched Dmitri's face closely while he read, feeling something akin to hope. He caught her eyes and stared intently, neither of them blinking. Then he smiled.

In the flurry of gift giving that followed, Aiyana saw a small notepad fall from Dmitri's cape. She knelt to pick it up and read the open page. *Fear surrenders in the sun: light, fire, force, life.*

Becky's Eyes

Becky turned when she heard Aiyana's voice from the parking lot. She and Kai waited for her to catch up, and they walked together to the gates of the Home for Children. Becky sighed deeply at the sun sparkling on the leaves still damp from the recent autumn shower.

Brian was already inside. Becky was pleased that both he and Aiyana had articles about their work accepted for publication. Brian's paper focused only on his energy theories while he reconsidered his covert methods of data collection. And Aiyana had excised all mention of prayer from her case studies. But Becky was still happy that each of her friends had birthed something from their soulful labors.

She finally met the nun who had held Dmitri close in her heart through all the years. Sister Catherine told them that he still hadn't spoken. She knocked on Dmitri's door then pushed it open. The modest room had what he needed but nothing more.

Dmitri was sitting on the bed. His red hair was clean and combed, and he was wearing a brand new, freshly pressed, purple cape. Becky thought he looked strange in it, not quite himself. He lifted his head when they came in. His stare was blank. The doctor had told them not to expect recognition.

While Dmitri opened his gifts, Kai set the baby carrier on the bed next to him. "We'd like you to meet Hope." Saying her daughter's name filled Becky with joy. As Kai lifted the little girl out of her seat, Becky saw a small notebook fall from his pants pocket. She read the open page. *Fear surrenders in the Son: light, fire, force, life.*

Acknowledgments

Thank you to Mom and Dad for your special blend of unconditional support and productive criticism.

Thank you to every friend, family member, and stranger who read my first book and encouraged me, directly or indirectly, to write another. This novel was rescued from the brink more than once by positive words that crossed my path at an opportune moment.

Thank you to the editors, writers, and more-than-just-readers who provided feedback on the "final" draft. Your honesty and thoughtful suggestions made this a better book, and I appreciate your time and insight.

Finally, thank you to the administrators and contributors at Indies Unlimited for your advice, encouragement, and camaraderie. This story floundered for years before your examples inspired me to, above all, keep writing.

Other Books by Krista Tibbs

The Neurology of Angels is a novel about the hearts inside the business and politics of drug development.

Reflections and Tails is an illustrated collection of short stories that reflect human lives through the animals that touch them.

Read excerpts and reviews at www.KristaTibbs.com.